LOCKDOWN

SCI-FI #3

Compiled & Edited by

Ben Thomas | D. Kershaw
Maggie Pawsey | S.N. Graves

Also available and coming soon from Black Hare Press

DARK DRABBLES ANTHOLOGIES

WORLDS
ANGELS
MONSTERS
BEYOND
UNRAVEL

APOCALYPSE
LOVE
HATE
OCEANS
ANCIENTS

BHP WRITERS' GROUP SPECIAL EDITIONS

STORMING AREA 51
EERIE CHRISTMAS

BAD ROMANCE
TWENTY TWENTY
SCHOOL'S IN

OTHER VOLUMES

DEEP SPACE
WHAT IF?
KEY TO THE KINGDOM
DEEP SEA

BEYOND THE REALM
BANNED
WETWARE

Twitter: @BlackHarePress
Facebook: BlackHarePress
Website: www.BlackHarePress.com

LOCKDOWN SCI-FI #3 title is
Copyright © 2020 Black Hare Press
First published in Australia in October 2020 by Black Hare Press

The authors of the individual stories retain the copyright of the works
featured in this anthology

*All characters and events in this publication, other than those clearly in
the public domain, are fictitious and any resemblance to real persons,
living or dead, is purely coincidental.*

Paperback : ISBN 978-1-925809-90-9

Cover design	Dawn Burdett	www.dmburdett.com
Formatting	Ben Thomas	www.blackharepress.com
Editing	D. Kershaw	www.blackharepress.com
	Maggie Pawsey	
	S.N. Graves	www.sngraves.com
Read Team	Alice Lam	
	David Green	davidgreenwritercom.wordpress.com
	H. Lynn Cornetto	
	Jennifer Hatfield	jhatfieldauthor.wixsite.com/website
	Jodi Jensen	jodijensenwrites.wordpress.com
	Lyndsay Ellis-Holloway	authorlyndseyellisholloway.webador.co.uk
	Stacey Jaine McIntosh	www.staceyjainemcintosh.com

TABLE OF CONTENTS

PEARLS THAT WERE HIS EYES

By Jen Downs

Tom Mallory watched fear twist the rookies' faces for an instant before the order to lock helmets. Forty-jump veteran Kessel wore a grin—he only came alive when he dived into the zone. The mission's first-timer, Brenner, awaited the 'go' light wide-eyed with dread. In the half-light behind her, Hal Kramer poised, cloaked in surreal calm, an old soldier who'd seen and done it all and didn't seem to give a cuss if he made it to the extraction or not.

Then Mallory dropped his visor along with the rest of Tango Company. Helmets locked, data immersed him like cool blue lake water while young Jo Brenner mumbled prayers. The transport wallowed over the zone now. They must jump low, hard, fall so fast through the flak, theoretically they'd bottom out with one chance in fifty of an individual taking a hit.

Forty *units* in Tango. Theoretically, they'd plummet through with zero casualties. Mallory often wondered who these theoreticians were, how they spun the numbers to derive such bullshine. Maybe

Command believed attractive odds softened the job for rookies on the 'virgin jump.' They could be right, but the theory made the truth no prettier.

After twenty jumps, Mallory's heart was a trip hammer. He took pity on Brenner with a gloved hand on her shoulder, but platitudes eluded him. *You'll be okay, kid, just stick close to me*—more bullshine. They all knew it, including Brenner.

Spinners, sirens. Data flashed red in the helmet display. A crazy whirl of sky and water—*jump!*

Mallory propelled Brenner ahead of him while Kessel dived out with a whoop and the veteran Kraemer launched serenely into freefall. Mallory envied the man's Zen, or Tao, whatever it was. He'd spent years hunting for the gift, but it might have been magic beans, or the grail. *You either got it or you don't, Master Sergeant Yip would say. And if you don't—*

Four seconds out of the transport, three of Tango became titanium shrapnel, carbon fibre confetti. For them, the Third Battle of the Murchison Deep ended in an instant. If the padres offered any more accuracy than the strategists, those kids just boarded the Valhalla Express with advance-booked tickets. Jo Brennan was one of them.

Encrypted comm from all viable Tango units thickened the air with shouting, whooping, demanding, begging, profaning, but red lights peppered Mallory's helmet display. He swore bitterly. Brenner, Munro, and Witherspoon were the lucky ones. Mallory himself was merely damaged.

He spun, tumbling after a glancing hit to the armour's back-mounted power pack. Data, visual and life support flatlined for several moments before the reserve cell kicked in, and then his eyes raced over the display while he fell like a brick through the last thousand meters to the wind-chopped surface of Endeavour Sound. Beneath him, Murchison Deep dropped away from the sun-bright line of the continental shelf.

Three times, this damn' battle had been fought. Five thousand servicemen and women had given their lives for this godforsaken expanse of water. Twice, Mallory had survived to reach a transport at the extraction point, and he knew the old superstition as well as anyone.

Third time's the charm, kid, he told himself while imitating a brick, well under the flak field now. The blue-green ocean raced up. He skimmed the instruments again and swore. The power pack was history. Backup provided just sufficient to start the beacon, in the insane hope the Corps might be victorious *enough* today for Recovery to launch in the clean-up.

He could be picked up in an hour or three. He repeated this as a mantra as he hit the sea. The armour absorbed most of the impact but his teeth rattled, blood's iron tang flooded his mouth. With the speed of impact, the suit plunged deep into dim green-grey, and he waited for flotation to kick in. If he had enough buoyancy to reach the surface, he'd start the beacon.

But the surface—where the G4 star formed a golden halo, great armoured batfish basked in its warmth, and squadrons of nautiloids flitted like motes in long, milky fingers of sunrays—continued to run away. Odd chills shivered around his left leg, and another swarm of red fireflies danced in his display.

Mallory groaned, beyond even cursing. "Suit's compromised," he muttered, talking to himself since power was too feeble to transmit in real-time. At least one smartseal had ruptured; part of the armour was taking water. Worse, the gas-feed to the flotation jacket had failed. "Sweet Christ," he whispered, less profanity than prayer, "I'm going down."

He thumped his left shoulder to release the beacon. It would mark his impact point, signal the transport. The tiny pod scudded upward, flare-bright yellow and already *pinging* among the curious nautiloids before he lost it in sun-glare. Then Mallory peered at his few functional instruments, trying to figure his rate of descent.

"Too fast," he whispered. Sweat prickled his ribs as he ran the numbers. The armour would protect him from compression as tonnes of water buried him. Even damaged, it cushioned him against the cold as he sank, but his body heat would rapidly bleed away through the already icy leg.

If he fell into the glacial deep and

Recovery took a long time coming, he could expect amputation if—an immense *if*—they found him at all.

"Tango three-four to Transport," he called repeatedly, uselessly. The beacon was sending; the transport's AI knew he was down as surely as it knew three *units* were reassigned to the posthumous honour roll before they dropped through the flak. "Tango three-four…" Talking to himself, perhaps in an effort to cling to sanity as the Deep took him.

Green dimness faded swiftly to black as he left behind sunlight, warmth, the welcome of surface waters where fisherfolk had encroached far enough to make Endeavour Sound seem friendly. The nearest landfall was a modest island on a chain of ancient volcanic peaks.

Ocean covered two-thirds of the world, and the last century had transformed the land into an open pit mine. This planet was about *resources*, not real estate. Ownership depended on who one asked. Mining rights belonged to Marsik Industries, according to lawyers forty floors up in Heidelberg Towers, on Tuesday. Ask any engineer on the *Hindmarsh Explorer* out of Franklin's World on Thursday. The result was war, long, bloody and bitter. Dominion over the Murchison Deep might be disputed for decades. These seas were littered with drifting hulks, the abandoned tech of forces from many corporate armies.

The futility had hit Mallory like a

punch months before. He was assigned here with a half year to serve before his compulsory enlistment was done. He would have shipped out with a fat wallet and authorisation to take another crack at life back home, all debts to society paid— lesson learned: *declare bankrupt, if you dare!*

Now, his back pay would go home in his stead, with the official letter. *Dear Mrs Mallory, it is with deep regret that we inform you of the death in action—*

He trusted the service to honour the contract, but life was a high price to pay for failure in business: a financial partner who vanished like smoke before he could be arraigned, taking two years' profits with him. Tom Mallory took the fall alone and was still falling…

He plunged into Stygian dark, shivering with the knowledge that the Deep formed a trench between immense mountain ranges. So many kilometres of water lay beneath him, the void between the stars seemed less overwhelming.

Surface comm traffic had faded to intermittent whispers; time was short if he intended to get any message out. Strictly, he should report to the Command AI, but he had a chance, given incredible luck, to transmit one micro-second data squirt. Nothing he knew would interest a strategist. He punched record and rasped, "Comm for Sylvia Mallory, listed next of kin. Priority. Message follows." He struggled his thoughts together, deliberately ignoring the dark. "Hey, Sylvie…I won't make it back after all. You were right, always are. Should've kept a closer eye on Carlo. Should've known he couldn't be trusted. Well, too late now.

"They'll let me tell you, I finished my tour at Murchison—didn't see any fighting this time. Got flakked as soon as I jumped. I'm in the water, going down, nothing under me but more water. They call it the *Deep*, right?"

He took a long breath. "Running outta time, can't send much more. I miss you, Sylvie. Thinking about you. The life we won't live together, all the things we won't do. Damn, I'm such a fool, like you always said. Tell our folks I'm thinking about them too. Love you, Sylv… Always did."

He blinked away smarting tears and focused on the instruments. He had fallen into the realm of slow, giant creatures out of nightmare. Thank gods such monsters were comparatively rare; nothing swam within sensor range. Life support might stretch to several hours, but his leg was cold-numb and felt crushed. The smartseal at the hip had held, or he'd have died minutes before, but he guessed he was bleeding from the foot. "Blood in the water," he whispered—in a realm of lamniformes the size of islands.

He closed his eyes, listened to the almost inaudible comm from the battle, the closer rhythmic, hypnotic *ping* of his own beacon, and the …

…shushshush-barrr-shush, barrrrrr-

shushshush-barrrr…

The odd sound jerked him back to awareness. His mind had begun to drift with shock and cold. The source was near, on a band close enough to his own comm for the armour's simple AI to register it. Not a voice, Mallory decided. More like the audible-spectrum white-noise of machine language.

He scanned down the comm menu, focused on *translate,* blinked to select. The helmet chip was rudimentary, but anything distracting him from the dark and cold was welcome. By comparison with a dedicated AI, the system was sluggish, dumb. He waited a half minute before it said, "Segrem 44, military encryption level 2."

What Mallory knew of machine

language was scant, but he recalled Segrem Laboratories as manufacturers of the best nano for military, medical and EM services, right back to Earth. "Dammit, *nano,*" he muttered. "A swarm of the buggers must be viable …"

Carried by the current from a wreck, or many wrecks. Suit sensors cranked to max. The exercise wasted life support potential, but he had no interest in spinning out a few grey, semi-conscious minutes at the end.

Vague forms loomed like ghosts in the murk, perhaps ships, aircraft, survival rafts, sunk, broken up and swept together like drifted snow. Murchison's deep, lazy gyre must end here.

"Neat," he whispered. "No strategic importance, not worth reporting even if I could, but—neat."

Drowsiness overtook him insidiously as shock, cold and blood loss conspired. The leg hurt right to the hip, and when his thoughts began to unravel, he was glad to let them.

With infinitesimal slowness he discovered he retained a thread of awareness. Some scrap of consciousness endured—enough for him to know his body thrummed—he felt sudden warmth, a growing dislocation, a tingling vertigo he recalled from the hospital a year before, when bionano rebuilt his spine.

Bionano. The buggers are in my blood, brain. Must've got in through the wound. Like microbes. Coherence eluded him. He might be dreaming, hallucinating with anoxia, afloat on the brink of clinical death. For all he knew, he might be dead already.

Thoughts formed languidly, without passion. All concept of time dissolved, but surely life support must have expired. Warmth enveloped him; or was it the absence of cold, or the loss of perception of cold? A tendril of mind pondered without urgency, watching, feeling, as his lungs spasmed at last in a long deep breath.

Water flooded them with the relief of oxygen, which should have been impossible, and yet—

Bionano embedded in his pulmonary alveoli fed oxygen to his starved lungs. Variants of this tech saved troops on the toxic battlefield. He drifted with fleeting awareness as bots stitched through his cells; but no Segrem engineer would have recognised this nano.

Mutated, he thought in a process of reasoning where a syllable spanned an hour. Military and medical 'bots had collided in this deep cold and, of necessity, swarmed in concert. They encountered life forms undiscovered by xenobiology. Dormant programs initialised. They multiplied, merged, laboured, collaborated on independent, undocumented projects; mutated again.

Tom Mallory's limbs tingled as, cell by cell, everything human perished and was repaired. Pain sparkled through muscle, bone, neuron, as biological molecules were painstakingly replaced with elements from the water that made the

Murchison Deep so precious, lives were sacrificed by the thousand in the battles to own it.

Downstream from the smoking volcanic chain of the Hades Mountains, this sea was so mineral-rich, filter-mining ships cruised like kilometre-long basking sharks. Fuel elements, medical isotopes—industrial vessels captured new, eccentric molecules which would one day cure a disease, armour a spacecraft, power a city. The prize was worth an ocean of human blood.

Blood, Mallory wondered, investing an hour in the speculation while swarming 'bots excised useless armour segments. *Do I have blood any longer?*

Titanium and carbon fibre fused into

his limbs. His shape spread, stretched, morphed. He was crystal, metal, plastex, rebuilt molecule by molecule as his living body failed. The pulmonary nano fed his lungs until his brain was more silicate and gold than biological.

And at last biological material was wholly absent, and Tom Mallory's mind cleared.

He took a deep breath, another, and gazed around with eyes perfectly suited to the dark. With integrated sensors, he saw much further. He felt a warm wind from Hades, which to the swarm meant nourishment, energy. He heard the *shushshush-barrr-shush* of the AI controlling the multitude with a muted data stream of Segrem 44—glimpsed the phantoms of four hulks, two of which coruscated with subtle energies.

I am Tech Support Tender 5 from carrier Baranov.

I am Medevac 3 from cruiser Hobart.

Both wrecks were serviced by their own swarms, which gorged on the bounty of the Deep, Mallory realised, years after these ships fell out of the sky. "I'm 85894 Mallory, T.R.," he sent via the chip salvaged from the armour, now fused into the back of his skull. "I'm alive."

Retrieval and repair is our function.

The swarm misted around him, a billion billion spores, milky in the cold darkness. Mallory kicked, felt the powerful surge of fins where living feet and armoured boots had once been. Heading up fast, he asked,

"Hobart Medevac, what am I?"

85894 Mallory functions, Hobart Medevac 3 said succinctly.

For the moment, it was enough. He took a bearing on the swarm and left it behind. A series of powerful kicks sent him into twilight waters which steadily brightened and warmed. His eyes contracted; his body adjusted to thermal and compression parameters without any conscious thought.

"Baranov Tech 5, did you install nano systems?"

Necessary for performance efficiency. Request report on function. Systems can be modified.

"I'm fine," Mallory told it as he rose into silver-blue light. He fanned out webbed hands with elongated digits, and at last thrust his head into air and moonlight. His lungs automatically spewed water before he took a deep gasp of warm air laden with the chemical reek of the Hades chain.

Four of the six moons rode between horizon and zenith, and millpond calm blanketed Endeavour Sound. To the north sprawled a ribbon of coastline, reefs and sand cays surrounding the cratered peak of an extinct volcano. The eastern sky burned brilliantly blue-black, almost cloudless.

His irises opened wide on the west, where the brightest stars sparkled in a last hint of peacock green. He saw no aircraft. Synthetic senses, fashioned from remnants of living brain and salvageable tech from the helmet, detected no comm traffic. Even the flak battery that reduced Tango to confetti stood dormant on the high shoulder of Mount Tartarus.

He stretched further and heard only faint whispers from a weathersat at geostationary, an abandoned surveillance drone in a decaying orbit. In a week, it would burn up.

The battle was so long over; the fleet had gone. Mallory couldn't hope to guess who'd won, who might return, and when. He knew only that he was alone in an ocean stretching far beyond every horizon—and 85894 Mallory *lived*. Of one thing, he was certain: if R&D glimpsed him, his next assignment was the lab. He would forfeit his liberty at once. Any ambition he owned would revolve around pain, and how to evade it.

Not yet. Perhaps eventually, if ownership of the Deep were decided by one army or another, he might announce himself. Share himself with humans when the hunger for company became worth a price paid in freedom and the inevitable suffering of the lab animal.

But not soon, though he was alone in an ocean without end, under utterly alien skies, and—

"85894 Mallory, hold position."

Signal direction was north/*down*. He caught his breath, spun toward the shore, where lazy combers rolled up a beach. "Who are you?"

A shape rose from the water, no larger

than himself, ambient at the temperature of the surface layers, as he was. Its shape was an amalgam of helmet and head, the face silver-black, glistening with pliant synthetic tissues. "62835 Kozachik, E.H., Lima Company, 242nd Marines, from the *Magellan.*"

Not a voice. Comm burst in his brain, as did transmissions from Baranov and Hobart. "Like me," Mallory murmured. *Transmitted.* "You were flakked out of the sky?"

"And rebuilt, like you." Kozachik finned closer. "Welcome."

"I...thanks, I guess." He knew he shouldn't have been surprised. It was arrogance, egotism, to assume he was unique, or the first. He felt the synthetic muscles of his face pull into a smile. "Hey, I can still smile."

"You can do many things." Kozachik was close enough now to speak aloud. His voice *(her* voice? Impossible to tell) rasped as if he rarely used it. Words seemed unforgivably slow to Mallory, measured against the thought-speed of direct comm.

He might have said this, but another shape surfaced a short way off; then another, and more. Instead, he said, "What are we?"

"New. More than we were born." Kozachik abandoned speech for comm, but a smile lifted one side of his/her mouth. "We won't go back. Only vivisection awaits. You desire weaponisation? Follow."

Two moons were setting as Tom Mallory finned after them. More like him rose from the calm waters of the sound. How many had Hobart and Baranov salvaged and rebuilt? He'd know soon enough, he thought. Eagerly, he followed his kind into blue-green moonlit grottoes, which to his new eyes seemed a garden of the gods.

First published in *Shorelines of Infinity #11*, 2018

LEFT INTO PARADISE

By David Green

All her years of sacrifice had finally paid off. Anna's golden ticket to Haven. Paradise, as everyone around her way called it. The ticket really was gold, too. Why use paper when such riches were so common? Word was they paved the streets with it. Surely a rumour ripped from some old-timey fairy tale, but Anna allowed her thoughts to wander where they would for once. She deserved that.

Her mind strayed to her family. That she wouldn't allow. *Useless wasters. Good riddance.* She'd done her very best to get away from those dead weights, who would do nothing but drag her back into the slums. With emotions like love. Empathy. She didn't have the time for any of that useless shite.

Anna had devoted her life to being the best athlete she could. It was the only way for people like her to get into Haven. Once a year, games of sport were held in each district around the protected cities. Events in running—long distance and sprint—climbing, fighting. Sometimes to the death.

Anyone in their eighteenth year had to take part. They invited the handful of the survivors to live in places like Haven.

Certainly, no-one ever came back.

Determined, Anna trained to be the best of the best. She'd kept her red hair short since she was a girl. Not to dissuade the attention of the boorish boys with their one-track minds, though that was a bonus. Anna was small and slight of build. Needed every advantage she could get—short hair meant less for an opponent to grab. She trained in being the fastest, the cleverest. In ways she could use her body to her advantage. She had won every event she'd entered. This ticket was her reward.

She didn't know why this was the way it was. Had been that way for years, and there weren't many old-timers around that could remember different. The righteous, wealthy citizens of Britannia lived their wonderful lives protected in their private utopias. Hidden away from the scum that invested the land. The only way in and out? Silver-and-gold-lined trains that hummed across monorails, crisscrossing the land.

The whole country was a giant, polluted, festering wound. Slowly smothering anything worthy like her. The only differences were the four protected cities, standing out like a stretch of clean skin on a beggar. There were *parks* in Haven. With trees! Anna had heard of four-legged companions people used to have. Dogs. She'd never seen one, but if there were any still alive, Haven would surely be the place they'd be.

A train was leaving today. Her ticket informed her she could pick any leaving over the next week. So she could say her goodbyes. *So civilised!* she thought. There would be no more trains for another year after that. Anna couldn't see any use in hanging around her sorry excuse for a home any longer. Family was done. She had little possessions.

First train it was.

The nearest station was an hour's run from where she lived. Anna fancied she could do it in half that time. She was the best, after all.

The platform was buzzing with excitement. Anna kept herself away from it. The stench was unbearable. Every day was a hot one, and most couldn't waste water to wash in. She knew she stank just as bad as everyone else baking under the sun's glare. The fiery bastard in the sky was shining its hardest on the pristine silver and gold train, too. The reflection so bright, Anna's green eyes stung when she tried to look at it. She didn't even see the lone figure emerge from the carriage doors in front of her until she heard his voice.

"Tournament winners! You are most welcome to leave your lives behind and enter Haven."

A man. Confident. Anna had tasted honey once, a long time ago. She fancied the voice's owner drank it by the gallon. Her stomach fluttered as she squinted to get a better look at him. Until she realised she'd look as gormless as the great unwashed on the platform. She strode on to the carriage without a second glance.

Another man was waiting.

"This one's keen, Charles!" The man called over her shoulder to his friend in that same cultured tone. "I'd imagine she'll be one to watch."

Anna had seen suits before. Suits that were clean. These men's were *gleaming*. Their skin was perfect, matching their hair with not a strand out of place. They even had full sets of white teeth.

"It is a fairy-tale," Anna breathed.

"All right, girl, move along. You're blocking your *friends* from their new life." The other man. Charles. A sardonic look on his superior face. "Come along Maurice, into the booth. We don't want any of this lot to touch us," he chuckled, slapping Maurice on the shoulder as they moved into an opaque partition.

Anna understood. She didn't want to be around her own kind any longer than she had to. She took up a position as close to the booth as possible, to overhear any conversation from the other side. The din from the tournament winners soon overwhelmed the idle chatter from the two strangers.

The carriage was crammed by the time the doors closed, the passengers standing elbow to elbow. The nervous excitement had turned to nerves alone as the train shot off on its journey. The only illumination coming from a few flickering light bulbs.

The smell of stale sweat, and God knows what else. A gentle sob from someone so overcome with emotion, trying desperately to not draw attention. A sense of foreboding.

Time passed, unmarked. It could have been days for all Anna knew. She could smell food from the partition occasionally. A scent from a rose, surrounded by shit. Her stomach growled, aching to be filled. Some other passengers had lost their footing and lay where they could. Some on top of others. Some held a companion for comfort. Just as Anna was about to give in and join them, some blessed relief from her complaining calves and feet, the train slowed to a stop. A tannoy crackled into automated life.

"PLEASE EXIT THE TRAIN TO THE LEFT IN AN ORDERLY FASHION.

WELCOME TO HAVEN."

The train was silent now, or Anna wouldn't have heard Maurice's low throaty laugh.

"Left into Paradise, dear boy. I always wonder if they have any inkling of what's coming."

The "winners" filed out into a clearing. It was the largest green space Anna had ever seen. She could see a tree line in the distance. Behind, and to the sides, was a towering, tiered seating section populated with spectators. Thousands of them. Underneath the seating were dozens of small gates. Too small for an adult to use. Something told Anna to fight her way to the front of the pack, to get as much distance between her and the gates as she could. The others fought back; they had the same idea. The throng struggled forwards to a sudden stop. She could hear fists and feet slapping, banging, scratching against glass. *What is this!?* Anna's mind screamed. A fairy tale turned nightmare.

On the other side of the glass, a podium emerged from the ground, flickering slightly. Behind it, an old woman in a gleaming white suit, vainly trying to hide her years behind a painted face. Her shrill voice boomed through the speakers surrounding them.

"Winners! You are welcome, most welcome indeed. Welcome to entertain us! Fight for us! Run for us! You are the best your *KIND* have to offer. SO, PROVE IT!"

The glass and podium disappeared

together as the gaggle stumbled forward as one. Shell-shocked. Some recovered and broke for the tree line. The woman was right, this was the best. Survivors one and all.

Anna was the best of them. She'd show them all. Shove the cries from the crowd into their perfect fucking faces. She jumped into a flat sprint until a sound brought her up short. A guttural yelp. Dozens of them. A constant, vicious bark. Anna looked behind her as lithe, graceful creatures emerged from the gates below the spectators. They were fast. There *were* dogs in Haven.

*****

From the safety of the train, Charles

watched with Maurice. The girl at the back of the pack stumbled. Fell. She sprang to her feet soon after; she was fast. No doubt about that. So were the dogs. They hadn't been fed in days.

"Looks like you were wrong, Maurice. This one won't last long. Pity, she seemed to hate her lot as much as I do."

"I'll bet you 1,000 that she'll get to the tree line." Maurice answered back, focused on the chase.

"Ha, you fool. You're on. She'll be caught in less than a minute." Charles' smile grew in satisfaction as the dogs closed in on her in half that time.

"Fuck it anyway," muttered Maurice. "Double or nothing. She's a fighter. It'll take the dogs over a minute to finish her.

Less than a minute, you'll get 2,000."

"Save it. There are always more poor people to bet on, dear boy." Charles replied, slapping Maurice on the shoulder as he headed back into the booth.

***

The cries of anguish and pain faded into the angry chatter of dogs fighting over scraps. The crowds headed home; the spectacle done for the day. Their departing buzz replaced with the hum of a train. A train speeding away to bring more lucky souls into Paradise.

PIECES OF GRACE

By Hari Navarro

One day the body of a beautiful naked woman appeared. She was dead—or at least it can be said she had not the animation of life. And her body contorted as it floated and wove through the air as if it were caught, hitched, on the very tip of a coddling breeze.

She was so fantastically beautiful that, at first, many thought she was not real.

Something this perfect, something this strikingly sexual had to be a construct.

A thing.

A thing made by man.

She first appeared in the desert. This, of course, emboldened the religious as they surmised that she must surely be heaven-sent. A fallen, broken, and lost angel, or perhaps even an errant daemon, and they pondered, and they fought over just what her message might be.

But then, as the curve of her breasts and the mound of her sex were giggled at by children and pushed behind the crucifix fingers of the pious, as her nudity consumed the minds of the masses, as she appeared on T-shirts and as she became the silent spokeswoman for a car insurance company, and as her image was redacted and then banned from billboards, the barest mention of her became... Well, it became quite suddenly...obscene.

Once obscene.

Never forgotten.

But still her gentle ballet traversed the globe entire, the folded back tips of her toes did drag through the sand, and the flay of her long limbs conducted the snow. She closed down major highways and curled gracefully through the driving rain, on and on and on and into the years.

Sometimes she'd elevate high up into the clouds and then spin and drift and plunge down into the sea. And it is here, away from the lights and from eyes that can only think to judge and condemn, here beneath the waves, alongside creatures and plants that moved as she, it was here, *here*, she revealed just what it was that she was.

What she was.

What she was for.

What she was here to give.

Scientists were the first to cut her. Initially, it was solitary strands of her hair that were plucked and the tiniest of cellular samples mined away from her core. We just had to know, you know? And then came the collectors, the hoarders, those hungry for souvenirs, and soon her beautiful floating hair became a gouged plain of bruises and scabs and cuts.

We shot her. Nobody knows who. But it's thought it was kids that put that tiny singed hole in her chest and the huge smoking cavern in her back. Kids can be cruel, don't they say that? Kids are the ones that are cruel?!

I think it's just that people had bored with her dance; they wanted more. They wanted revelation, but it never came. So they picked, and they prodded at her seams till she broke.

We broke her.

We broker her.

Even now, after all this time, pieces of her come up at auction. There's a guy in Hong Kong that owns a near completely intact left leg. They're really sought after, and there's even talk now of gathering them all up and trying to piece her back together. They can do that sort of thing now, or so I'm told.

And maybe, then, we'll know.

Maybe then we'll know just what it was she was for.

First published on *365tomorrows.com*, 2019

THE APOLLO CONTAINMENT

By James Pyles

When Astronaut Eugene Downey sneezed, it heralded the beginning of the end, although years later, everyone involved would consider it a new beginning, albeit born of tragedy.

"What the hell, Gene?" Naval Commander Norman Peters patted the Command Module pilot on the back as if burping a baby. "Cake got stuck in your nose?"

"Maybe I'm allergic to your birthday, Norm…or your jokes." Gene looked up at the mission commander from his kitchen chair.

"You two are lucky the press isn't still out there recording all this through that observation port." Nodding at the heavy Plexiglas window behind him, Tom Martin chuckled, while sitting at the oblong aluminium table across from Gene, scooping up a final bite of ice cream.

"We're just lucky our wives and kids aren't here to see you pass angel food cake up your sinuses." Norm Peters was internationally famous as the commander of the Apollo 14 mission to the Moon, but less renowned for his ill-timed sense of humour. "If we have to spend ten more days locked down in this tin can, at least you can enjoy my wife's cake."

"Norm, this is Dr Bowen." The voice of NASA's medical officer, in charge of their three-week quarantine after their return from the Moon, crackled over the intercom. Three heads turned as if on one swivel, toward the large hatch leading from the mobile isolation facility's kitchen to the sequestered medical pod on the other side.

"Oh, come on, Doc," Peters complained, still trying to laugh. "It was just a..." He felt Downey standing up next to him. Norm let his hand drop and looked at Gene. He seemed paler than just an hour ago when the press conference ended. That was saying something, since Downey had inherited the totality of his mother's Irish red hair and freckles. "Sorry, Gene."

"Probably your wife just put too much vanilla in the frosting. I'm sure I'll be fine."

"Gene, I need you to go into your quarters and sit at the bio-desk. I want to take a complete set of readings on your current condition."

"On my way, Doc."

Thirty-eight-year-old Gene Downey turned away from Bowen's voice to the opposing hatch and headed deeper inside the titanium reinforced structure. Tom stood up and moved next to Norm as they watched him open the passage into their shared living quarters.

"You gentlemen have to take this

seriously." Bowen lectured them like a stern father. "You know you were kept quarantined for three weeks prior to launch, monitored for every medical condition we know about. I personally assured the President and the Director of NASA that each one of you didn't have so much as a hangnail prior to liftoff."

"Yeah, and Gene doesn't have any allergies," Tom muttered. He turned and saw Norm blushing. They had become close in the two years since they were selected for the Apollo 14 mission. They shared just about everything, birthdays, their kids' baseball games, wedding anniversaries, they were bonded like brothers. Being military officers, that bond included a lot of male-fuelled kidding around.

They knew that the quarantine for the crews of the previous three Apollo missions had been routine, nothing unusual. NASA hadn't expected this one to be any different, and there was talk of stopping the practice altogether for future flights.

"It's probably nothing." Tom patted the Commander on his shoulder, inadvertently tousling Peters' dark brown hair across his forehead. At nearly 50, Apollo 14's mission leader could easily have been passed for a man of Tom's or even Gene's age. Irrationally, Martin lamented his own almost hairless pate, though thankfully he wasn't a complete cue ball like Bowen.

"Yeah, probably nothing, but let's go find out."

***

"So what the hell is going on, Bowen?"

"I'm a little busy treating my patient, General." At six foot six, Morris Bowen felt cramped in the Spartan confines of the astronaut isolation quarters. He was hunched over Gene, who was lying on his bunk, taking the Captain's vitals for the fifteenth time that morning.

"Bowen, I'm not a patient man."

The doctor spun his head to the right, dislodging his stethoscope, facing the observation port, privacy curtains drawn wide. He grimaced at the four-star Air Force General who had military jurisdiction over NASA in this crisis. "I'm a doctor first, General Richardson. My patient is sick, and I don't know what's causing it. When I get a news flash, I'll let you know."

"Hell, it's bad enough you exposed yourself to whatever this is, but the rest of your team…"

"…are volunteers and critical medical support personnel. We all knew what could happen…"

"To hell you did. Every other Apollo containment was a cakewalk. After Apollo 11, no one saw anything like this coming."

"Which is why my staff and I need to be in here, closely examining this medical anomaly."

In a huff, the giant of a man gently replaced his earpieces and resumed listening to Downey's accelerated heartbeat.

Thaddeus Richardson gritted his teeth, wishing he was allowed to smoke a cigar in Houston Space Centre's secured medical building. "Can you at least tell me why Peters and Martin aren't displaying symptoms?"

"We're right here, General. Don't talk past us like we're not." Norm was standing next to the observation window, but facing away from Richardson, mournfully looking at his unconscious comrade. He glanced over to the right at Tom who was sitting on his bunk just a few feet from

Downey. The Lunar Module pilot gave the impression of a child who was mourning a dead parent.

"Commander Peters, I remind you…"

Bowen cut the General off. "Talk to my staff. They're analysing the latest results. Fuller, Johnson. tell the General the latest results, and have Carpenter come in here."

"Right away, Doctor."

Richardson recognised Roosevelt Johnson's voice over the open mike. He was the senior medical tech on the project. It was an assignment he personally disagreed with, but the Washington bigwigs said having a black professional present would help NASA's public image, especially with civil rights leaders.

"Well, Johnson?"

"Just a second, General." They heard hushed tones over the speakers, "He wants you in there."

"Right away." Nurse Megan Carpenter's response was a momentary calm in a sea of churning chaos.

They could hear Johnson speaking in whispers to the other tech, Larry Fuller, for a moment. "Sorry for the wait, General. Teletype just came out with the latest results from the mainframe.

"And…?"

"I'm here, Doctor." Carpenter entered through the open hatch. Graduated top ten in her class, two tours of duty in a Vietnam surgical unit, unmarried at 33, career Army. She was a stoic anchor in traditional nurse's white, complete with accompanying ridiculous hat. Peters and Martin enjoyed the relative comfort of being attired in loose, blue jumpsuits, though at the moment, it hardly mattered.

"Thanks, Megan. Take the patient's B.P. again.

"Johnson?"

"Frankly, rows of supercomputers and the best medical experts in the country are still stumped. We know that Captain Downey's biological processes are undergoing a radical change. His lungs are 20 percent less efficient at processing oxygen, but there's some indication that he might be capable of respiration of a thicker medium, possibly liquid."

"Water?"

"We're not sure yet. Besides that, his eyes are showing characteristics of vision outside the usual visual wavelengths. Without testing, we can't be certain, but possibly he could see into the infrared and ultraviolet range."

"What the hell does it all mean?"

"Well…" Johnson's voice faded, and there was some background murmuring as he consulted Fuller.

"It's okay, gentlemen. We discussed this earlier with Commander Peters and Lieutenant Martin." Bowen kept his attention on Downey while still quietly giving Carpenter instructions.

"Yes, sir. Well, on a fundamental level, we believe Captain Downey is no longer human."

"What?" The General took three steps backward. Despite being near retirement age, he was as fit as any man in the Air Force, but betrayed by a voice that sounded like a cement mixer, and close cropped hair the colour of shale. "A little Moon dust did all that?"

"We don't know the transmission vector, General Richardson. We only know what we can observe," the Doctor mused, still examining Downey.

"Why aren't Peters and Martin affected, or are they?"

"We've run the same tests on them as we have on the Captain. They show no signs of this bizarre…metamorphosis. We don't know anymore about that than we do about why Downey is changing."

"I want to see her!" Gene lurched up spasmodically, forcing Bowen and Carpenter to pull back to avoid his head crashing into them.

"Son, it's alright." Bowen put his hand gingerly on the astronaut's chest, trying to ease him back down. Tom stood, looking over Megan's shoulder while Norm took a step toward the bed.

"Let me see her. I've got to…" He started blurting out words that became an incomprehensible whisper, like mumbling in the dark.

"That isn't English, Doctor. What's he saying?"

"Beats the hell out of me, Megan. Help me get him down again."

"He wants to see his wife. Can't blame

him. We all wish…" Martin cut himself off, biting his lip against the anguish.

Norm turned to the window. "What have you told our families about this?" He waved an arm excitedly in Gene's direction.

"They only know what we let the rest of the world know."

"What idiotic story…?"

"Commander, we couldn't inform the public about the situation. It would destroy the space program, ruin America's image."

"To hell with America's image, General. What have you told our families?"

"We...uh, leaked to the press that you were in isolation due to a covert military operation you conducted on the Moon." For once, the brash General seemed almost contrite.

"Didn't we sign a treaty preventing anything like that? Do you think anyone will believe…?"

"Oh, the Soviets are having kittens about it, Peters. They believe it alright, and so does everyone else."

"This is to protect America's reputation? You've cast us in the role of an imperialist superpower, ignoring our own laws and treaties when it serves our interests." The words left Norm's lips with the realisation that, no matter how pathetic Richardson's lie, the broader implication was the complete truth.

"Doctor!"

"Yes, I see it, Megan."

"See what?" Tom leaned closer to the

nurse. She flinched as his hot breath was exhaled against the back of her neck.

"His eyes. Good thing we're keeping the lights low. He'd probably have been blinded otherwise."

"Captain Downey's fingers."

"Yes, and his skin. He's continuing his metamorphosis."

"General, that cover story of yours."

"What about it, Martin?"

"Is it just a cover story?"

"Tom, what are you talking about?" Norm had the look of a concerned older brother watching a sibling about to fall off a ledge. "You and I were together on the Moon. We followed mission parameters to a T".

"What if the brass knew something

about the Fra Mauro formation…the crater? No other mission explored such a structure before."

"We never even made it to the crater."

"But we brought back some ejecta from it, material none of the other missions had retrieved. What if NASA or the Pentagon knew what was up there, knew it could be weaponized? A biological agent."

"That's a little too much 'Andromeda Strain,' don't you think, Tom?" Gene took another step toward Martin, as he became more agitated. Megan chanced a brief peek back at him. Bowen looked out the port at the General who was subtly signalling the two MPs forward, not that it would do them any good. Besides the medical team, no one was allowed into the quarantine trailer by direct order of President Nixon.

Dr Bowen felt a tight pressure on his left forearm and looked down to see Gene's claws, now covered with fine blue-green scales, a thin membrane of webbing between them, seize his flesh in an icy grip.

"Got to see her."

"Gene," he murmured. "We can't let you see your wife right now. We still have to determine what's causing…"

"Bertha, damn it! Bertha! She's the key. She always has been. Bring her to me."

"Is this what you wanted, General? Is this why we've been sacrificed."

"Tom, I…"

"You aren't in command now, Norm!" Martin shook the other man's hand off his shoulder and pushed him back. "Isn't this what you wanted?" Tom rushed to the port and slammed both fists violently against six-inch thick Plexiglas. "Isn't it???"

General Richardson knew each of the three Apollo astronauts as well as he did his own sons. He knew part of the reason they'd been chosen for the program was because they had demonstrated the ability to remain calm and in control, even under tremendous stress. Like the others, Martin had been both a combat and a test pilot. He could look an enemy in the eye and never blink.

But now the enemy wasn't an aircraft or another fighter pilot. It wasn't even human.

"He's not talking about his wife,

Doctor. Her name is Janice." Norm cautiously walked closer to Tom, who was still pressed up against the glass. "Big Bertha's what we named that big rock specimen."

"I've had all of those rocks examined. So far, no pathogen's been detected, nothing that could have infected Downey, or you two. As far as Big Bertha's concerned, the only thing…but it's ridiculous."

Bowen pulled abruptly away from Gene. "You found something relevant and didn't inform me?"

"The geology team didn't think…"

"Damn it, General. The geology team aren't medical professionals. What did they find?"

"Some sort of pattern or design."

"Have the results sent over, and I mean right now!" Bowen was standing, fists balled, as if Martin's rage had been transmitted through the air into his heart. Tom was still tense, but he let Norm pull him to one side, away from the window.

Richardson gritted his teeth. If this were any other situation, he's have snapped Bowen from Lt. Commander back to Seaman first class, and never mind that they were in different branches of the service. But Bowen was the best man for the job, and the General knew he was way out of his league, insubordination be damned.

"Don't get your knickers in a wad, Doctor. I'll have the data sent to you at once." He nodded over his shoulder, and one of the M.P.s turned on heel and double-timed it across the hanger floor toward the nearest exit.

***

Martin chose to stay with Carpenter and Fuller, watching over the continually mutating body of Gene Downey, while Dr Bowen, along with Peters and Johnson, were in the medical research compartment. They were pouring over the data stored in the experimental Compaq 640 computer module, it's eight-inch monitor crowded with equations.

General Richardson, and an anonymous collection of top military officers, scientists, and Presidential advisors, tuned in remotely under the tightest security since the Manhattan Project.

"This, gentlemen, is the reason the geological team was unable to decipher these patterns." Johnson balanced the grim intensity of the information he was examining against the phenomenal unlikelihood of a young black man from Detroit being at the centre of a project of global significance. He wanted to be proud as one of the top graduates from Stanford in Genetics Research, but, for the moment, he savoured finally being one of the team.

"It's a DNA helix."

"Yes, Doctor, but a highly specific one."

They could hear a crackle over the speaker, and then General Richardson uttered a single, inarticulate syllable. After that, the noise died down.

"It matches, as best as we can map with current technology, the genome we're seeing emerge in Captain Downey."

"But not precisely, Doctor. Look here and here..."

"Uh huh. I see. Points of attachment, as if..."

"As if they are two parts of a larger whole."

"But what does it add up to, Bowen?" Richardson still didn't want to acknowledge that Johnson was more of the expert in this context than the chief medical officer.

"If I'm understanding this right, it's not just strands of DNA we're seeing. It's some sort of code...or map."

"I'm just eyeballing this, Doctor. It'll take hundreds of hours of computation to confirm it, but I think we may be looking at a set of coordinates, to where I'm not sure."

"I'm sure." Peters, standing behind Johnson who was working at the keyboard, put his hand on the scientist's chair back and leaned over. The blue-white strobe flickering in his eyes held the answers to a myriad of mysteries. "It's a set of coordinates in space, at least part of it is."

"Where?"

"Unless I miss my guess, General, it's near the orbit of the planet Uranus."

"But what's the rest of this data?

There's too much here to be just spatial coordinates."

"That's what the experts out here think too, Bowen."

"Do they have any ideas about the rest of what we're seeing, General?"

"Look closer, Doctor. I think it leads back to our patient."

"You're right, Roosevelt. The end result, if there is such a thing."

"Of what?"

"Of what Captain Downey is mutating into, General." Bowen stood and looked in the direction of the CCTV camera on the far wall past the computer consoles. "An alien intelligence. I know this sounds crazy, but so does everything that's happened in the past few weeks. I think whatever Apollo 14 brought back from the Moon, specifically the Big Bertha rock sample, was designed as a form of communication. Something not of this Earth planted a seed on the Moon ages ago."

"The Fra Mauro formation is estimated to be 4.25 billion years old, and created by some sort of massive impact," Peters interjected. "What if some otherworldly intelligence put the equivalent of a message in a bottle on the Moon that long ago. They may have been waiting for a species on Earth to evolve intellectually, and then become space travellers."

"You were all exposed to the same artifacts from the Moon once you and

Martin returned to the command module. Why was only Captain Downey affected?"

"Your guess is as good as ours at this point, General," Bowen answered. "It might be as simple as being allergic to a bee sting. Only about five to seven percent of the human population has that susceptibility. It could be the same with whatever the aliens deposited on the Moon."

"So you think that these aliens left us both a schematic of their biology, literal and symbolic, as well as a map to their front doorstep?"

"More like an outpost, General."

"Peters?"

"I can't imagine a form of life naturally evolving on or near Uranus."

"I'd have to agree based on my examinations of Captain Downey. As radical as they appear, there's nothing to indicate he is related to any form of being that could endure the extreme conditions we understand to be characteristic of that gas giant."

There was more static across the speakers, a collection of low voices consulting. "So an invitation, then. They want to meet us on what amounts to neutral ground in our own solar system, rather than tip their hand as to their true point of origin."

"A lot of conjecture, I admit, General. We'll have to continue examining the data to draw more definitive conclusions, and that could take years."

A red lamp flashed frantically next to the hatch leading into the astronaut quarters. "Doctor Bowen, hurry!" Megan's voice hissed over the intercom, and then was carried out to those few additional souls privileged to be part of the greatest puzzle in the history of humanity.

Bowen raced through the passageway first, followed by Norm. Roosevelt looked back at the information he'd been examining, especially the latest data about Downey's transformation. He knew before the experts at NASA what Bowen was about to find.

***

Retired Air Force General Thaddeus

Richardson was over seventy years old when he stood crowded among the sweaty throngs outside of Cape Canaveral, watching the launch of the Voyager 2 probe. It was August 20, 1977, over six years after the tragic death of Captain Eugene Brian Downey, or whatever he had been changing into before his valiant heart gave out under the strain. Officially, he had died in a covert military test flight along with his fellow astronauts Norman Peters and Thomas Martin. The reality was somewhat more gruesome, and even Captain Downey's widow and children would never know the truth.

What Gene Downey had become was still locked away in a covert laboratory sixty feet beneath the sands of Groom

Lake, Nevada, a location the public fancifully referred to as Area 51. For once, the tabloids got it right. There really was an alien hidden there from prying eyes.

Peters and Martin were still very much alive near the same location, and as far as a team of medical and scientific experts were concerned, healthy, if not particularly happy. They had company, though. Bowen, Johnson, Fuller, and Carpenter had all been exposed. Fortunately, the Weather Underground Organisation chose March 1, 1971, to detonate a bomb in one of the men's rooms at the United States Capitol. Dr Morris Bowen and three other NASA medical staff, present for a private meeting with the Congressional Administrator of the space agency, were killed in the explosion, their bodies rendered unrecognisable. That was the official story, anyway.

As Richardson tilted his head back, watching enormous thrust push the Titan-Centaur rocket past the two-mile mark, he remembered his last visit with them. He saw with his own eyes that they were all still wholly human. A fleet of medical experts said that every one of them also showed signs of a massive infection, the effects of which they were completely immune. Only roughly seven percent of the human race could be changed by the Fra Mauro virus. So those brave Americans, the six finest heroes with whom the General had ever served, had to remain forever sealed in containment, locked down in a gilded, steel pen, alone for the sake of the rest of the world.

"Godspeed, Captain Downey." Only a few among the press of tourists and spectators noticed the old man solemnly saluting the rapidly vanishing spacecraft. "You never asked for the honour, but you gave your life in the performance of your duty, a sacrifice not only for an unknowing nation, but for all of humanity."

He relaxed his arm as the fire trail dissipated. Hours later, he was standing alone on the same spot, still staring at the same piece of darkening sky where Voyager 2 had left the confines of the atmosphere.

"In eight and a half years, almost exactly fifteen years after Downey died,

Voyager and our message will reach you."

It had always been meant to perform its "grand tour" of the solar system, including a Uranus flyby. But because of the astronauts of Apollo 14, the space probe had an additional, if clandestine, purpose. It was the vanguard of humanity, our olive branch, the planet Earth's response to the alien invitation.

"We're here," Richardson uttered. "We listened to you. We've been alone, isolated on our own little world for our entire existence. We're ready to come out and join you. We're waiting."

STAIRS TO THE SKY

By Joanna Michal Hoyt

This is the first sequence from the stairway's history that we've been able to retrieve. The people surrounding the structure stare at it with evident bewilderment, suggesting this may be their first glimpse of it. The place from which the stairway rises is probably not unfamiliar to the onlookers; the market stalls scattered across the field appear weathered. Most of the stalls are unattended. Those few proprietors who have stayed put lean across their counters, staring at the stone steps that spiral upward, turning clockwise, almost as far as the eye can see, ending at a dizzy height.

How high is it? Someone is pacing out the length of the shadow that extends westward from the market across the plain. The sun is low. The measurer's shadow is at least twice as long as he is tall. Will he calculate the ratio of his shadow to his own height and reduce his tower-height estimate accordingly? Impossible to tell, since this first sequence is without sound.

Most people are looking at the tower itself. Wondering, perhaps, not *How many feet high is it?* but *How many steps would I have to climb to reach the top?* or, *Where did it come from?* or, *Is there anything on top?*

An old woman begins to climb, followed by a young man. They ascend slowly, left hands against the central stone column into which the narrow end of each wedged step melts with no visible joint. It must have occurred to them that there is no wall or railing on the outside and the fall would be very long.

The old woman reaches the top, where the stair ends in a semicircle of smooth stone. She turns, gazing southward over the wind-tossed grass and the scattered houses, northward to the hills, westward to the dimly glimpsed mountains, eastward across the flatland toward the far gleam of sea. Then she looks into what appears to be empty sky. Her eyes focus on something close by, something we can't see. She takes one more step upward and ahead, over the edge, setting her foot down firmly on thin air, and then she is gone.

She is gone. Not fallen—at least, we do not see her falling, and afterward there is no bone-crazed huddle at the tower's foot. The young man, who had reached out to steady her, let his arm fall. Looks where she looked. Begins the long climb down.

***

1.

The docent couldn't, or wouldn't, explain how these "sequences" were obtained. I've read about Dr Weltanschauung's "psycho-refractive image/sound recovery," about the "sequences" she takes at historic or symbolic sites where she believes some kind of localised retrievable memory-record of events exists, but then don't explain how it works. The docent said this exhibit was designed to display records of historical or anthropological interest, and technical methodology was in the domain of another department. I suppose that means she doesn't know.

Monica insisted on replaying the last minute of the first sequence three times, checking whether there was anything under the old woman's feet as she vanished, or any sign that the sequence had been tampered with. I suppose now they could engineer it to look perfectly natural. Some people say this entire exhibit is a fake—or, more charitably, a work of art inspired by the strangeness of that stairway.

***

B.

The market stalls are gone. The stairs rise solitary from the grassland, casting a shortened shadow eastward. One figure stands atop the high platform, huddled under a thick hooded cloak. The watcher's face swings from the broad expanse of wind-bent grass to the sky with its hurrying clouds, then downward and eastward, seaward...

The far line of sea bunches, swells. A small patch of silver lifts like a banner, flaps against the dark clouds on the horizon. Then the whole line of water rises smoothly, surges closer. The watcher clasps hands to mouth, scrambles down with desperate caution, runs southward toward the houses, falls, rises, runs again.

For a while, the grassland around the tower is empty. Then people begin to pass. First a few riders, then many runners and walkers, carrying bundles or children toward the northern hills. As the sun sinks to the western horizon a smaller company comes on foot, stumbling, limping. They must have decided—wisely—that they can't make it to the hills. They drag themselves up the stairs. They have almost reached the top when the gold-gleaming water glides over the grass, smooth except where its surface is disturbed by planks, branches, bodies of sheep and men. It rises past the eighteenth stair, and there it remains, churning and sucking, through the evening and the slow hours of the night, while the refugees shiver on the stairs. In the first grey light of morning, the water begins to recede.

***

C.

Later again. There is a small open area around the tower's foot; beyond that is a sprawl of stone buildings with arched doorways. The people gathered in the open space wear bright-hued fringed clothing. There's sound now, excited murmurs, solemn tones of people holding forth, and, away eastward, a sound of singing. As the singing grows louder the crowd-noises fade and the song, modulating steadily higher and higher, would be intelligible to anyone who knew the language.

The singing comes from a small group walking in single file, dressed in plain white clothing, fringeless. They have little in common besides their attire: there are youths, elders, women, men. Some stride confidently; some shuffle; one limps. The leader, the limping man, stands still in front of the first stair. The singing stops. The crowd falls silent. Then, as he begins to climb, as the other white-robed ones follow him, saving their breath for the ascent, the crowd takes up their song, starting at a low pitch, rising.

The short file winds upward. The watchers raise their arms toward them, lift the song higher. Their faces are intent. One or two tip their heads from side to side and bite their lips as though struggling toward a decision.

In the back of the crowd an expressionless woman stands watching the leader, not singing. The boy on her shoulders weeps.

The leader reaches the high platform and, like the woman in our first glimpse, looks around. He raises a hand, perhaps to the weeping boy, who waves frantically. Then he steps up into the air and is gone.

One after another they follow him.

The next to last turns and steps up like all the rest, strides into empty space, falls like a stone. Someone tries to run to her. Others grasp the runner's arms.

She lands head-foremost, is dead at once. The crowd still sings. Some keep their eyes on her while others watch the last climber vanish into the sky. Then they all gather round her. Someone has a stretcher; such things must have happened before. They sing as they bear her away.

***

2.

After the woman landed, when we saw her close up again, her head was so badly damaged that she had no expression. But Monica made the docent show her fall again. For a second while the woman fell, her face was turned toward us, and she was smiling.

Peter said that proves she was an actor, the whole thing never happened.

But what if it's real? What if she did fall, and did smile?

***

D.

Later again. The stone buildings near the stairway look old and neglected. Away eastward higher buildings rise. The crowd at the base of the stairs is silent. All the people are dressed darkly and plainly. They are gathered round the stairs again, but at a greater distance. Guards—armed men, at any rate, looking variously impressive and uneasy—stand in a ring around the stairs, facing outward, though it is not clear that any of the onlookers would wish to approach the stairs more closely if permitted.

The party which draws all eyes approaches from the west, along the tower's shadow. Four armed guards, and between them a tall young man, unarmed, dressed as darkly and as plainly as the crowd. The young man's eyes move from the tower to the crowd and back again.

One of the armed men stands forward, speaks briefly. His inflection is formal, although his words are unintelligible. The crowd does not move or speak. The young man nods to them before his guards herd him onto the bottom stair. Only one guard follows as he begins to climb.

They mount, the guard always four stairs behind, until the young man stumbles—no, casts himself down, bracing his knee in the tread of the stair above, jabbing at the guard's groin with his other foot. The guard falls over the edge and crumples on the ground. Thrashes. They weren't so far up, maybe twice the guard's height, and he fell legs down. He's trying to sit up. Two of his fellows bend over him while the other hurries after the dark-cloaked young man, who is still climbing. Whatever he intended, it wasn't escape.

The relief guard is still several turns

from the stairhead when the young man reaches the top and lifts his foot gingerly, seems to feel for something. His toe curls down over the edge of the platform. He frowns. Looks up. Shrugs. Takes one great stride over the edge and vanishes into the bright air. Some of the watchers shift their eyes downward as soon as he steps out; they look back up when it becomes clear that he has not fallen.

As the crowd disperses silently, a few of them thrust their arms up in a half-fierce, half-furtive gesture toward the sky.

***

E.

A sickle moon in the grey night. Even

in this half-light the buildings on the plain around the stairway's base are unmistakably long abandoned, crumbling. The wind blows through the ruins, whistles in the empty window arches, moans around the pillar. The wind makes the long grasses bow, shakes the rough stems of knapweed and thistles.

Something else moves in the waste. Someone, rather. A figure muffled in a long coat crouches behind sagging walls, scuttles across open spaces, moves in stops and sudden darts toward the tower. Only a hundred yards away. Only a hundred feet away. Only three paces...

Another figure, armed, springs out from behind the tower, seizes the furtive one's arm. Whispers unintelligibly, but someone has worked out a translation, for a subtitle appears:

"Bloody fool. Go back. I won't report you. This time."

The other does not answer. Stands still and silent until released. Raises one arm toward the tower top. Turns, strides away against the wind.

***

3.

"Is it guarded now?" I asked.

The docent shook her head. "Who has money for that?"

***

F.

Much later. The noise from the city to the east suggests motorised traffic. The distant buildings are blurred with smoke and heat-haze. A small group of people are busy near the stairway. The old stone structures that once surrounded it are almost entirely flattened. Four people hunt for stones in the tangled grass, make notes, call back and forth. Four more stand in the shadow of the stairway, looking up. One gestures upward. They all talk at once, and we can understand them.

"...ritual purposes, probably, or perhaps an observatory..."

"...a stunning view, I suppose, when the air was clearer..."

"...certainly an odd style of stonework,

and not the local stone either..."

"...do you suppose it's safe?" This last question comes out in a pocket of silence.

"Safe?"

"To climb. It doesn't look like the strongest design..." The speaker sounds embarrassed: by his timidity? or by the fact that his initial question had another, less answerable meaning?

"It's held up all this time."

"But no one's been up it in..."

"...dog's years."

"Your precise grasp of scientific terminology never fails to awe me."

The next-to-last speaker grins and starts to climb, counting the stairs as he goes. At the top he examines the flat platform, turns to take in the view, makes notes, climbs back down. "Six hundred steps," he says. "Quite uniform. Nothing at the top. No inscription, no picture, not even a sighting line."

The sound fades out. The party moves away to examine the fallen buildings.

***

4.

That's right. That's how my great-uncle told it. He liked repeating the bit about dog's years.

If they made this up—if they did it with actors—they could make things fit like that.

***

G.

Daylight. The people walking across the mown grass from the car park at the edge of our viewing frame wear contemporary clothing. Four women, three men, carrying folding easels, picnic-baskets, thermoses, backpacks, binoculars.

"You took your sweet time getting started. See, we've lost the best of the light already."

"Don't whinge so. You're the one who kept us up last night, trying to get the best of the moonlight."

They disperse. One settles on the west, or sunward, side, sets up her easel, unpacks a paint-box. Another sits with his back to the stone of the wall, pulls a notebook from his backpack, starts to write. The rest climb up the stairs to varying heights, sit down and start to write or draw. Most stop well below the halfway mark. The whinger ascends, panting, to the very top before unpacking her sketchpad. She sits cross-legged, her back to the sun and her face to the far-off sea, looks out for a while, opens a box of coloured pencils and begins to draw. She works intently for a long time, bending so low over the page that her picture is hidden. Then she stretches, sets the pad down and fossicks in her backpack.

"Oy! Selene!" the painter at the bottom shouts. The artist at the top looks down.

"What now?"

"What are you doing with your sketch pad?"

"I just set it down."

"On the air?"

"On the stone! I didn't drop it, I set it down...I felt it..." Her voice rises a bit as she pats the stone behind her, turns around, realises the sketchbook isn't there. She sighs. "I must have bumped it."

"Where is it, then?"

"You must have seen where it fell."

"It didn't fall," the painter says. "It disappeared."

"Of course it didn't." Selene frowns. "I can't see the ground right around the tower from here..."

The painter circles the staircase, finding nothing, and calls to the others in the party. No one has seen Selene's sketchbook. It's nowhere. It's gone.

***

5.

Moonlight again. I stand at the smooth platform at the top of the stairs, the place I have imagined since I heard Great-uncle Mark's stories, the place I have dreamed about since I saw Weltanschauung's sequences. I didn't dare come here till today. I'm not sure what I was afraid of finding, or not finding.

Nor am I sure what I have found. The stone is cold. The wind is cold. The stars are streaming fire. In the hour since I finished the climb, I've twice thought I saw the next step gleaming in the air. In between times it seems clear there's nothing there.

I've felt the air where they stepped out, and I can't feel anything. I put my book bag on the empty space where Selene's sketchbook was. It fell. Just as well; it has my non-suicide note inside, in case this night never appears in the mirror of memory. I still have my notebook to record any last thing I may see...

They won't need to find this or my note if I act sensibly and come back down.

But twice I saw the starlight catch on something just beyond the edge...

There, there it is. I'm going.

First published in *Summer 2017 Anthology*, Holdfast Magazine, 2017

ONE DISSONANT INTERVAL

By Beth W. Patterson

Technically, she was luring them to their deaths. If she died in the process, it still might be worth it. The thought was the one consolation Wurli could cling to in her absolute terror during lift-off.

The entire spacecraft swayed so violently, it felt to her like it might burst apart. She was physically untrained for space flight and had no idea what to expect. Through the window, she watched the explosions on the Blue Planet get further and further away. The ship's velocity pinned her to her seat; she only had the strength to roll her eyes at her two crewmates or watch the sky ahead darkening as the atmosphere thinned. The fourth member of her party was nowhere to be seen, and she couldn't imagine he'd survived.

She wished she could watch the destruction of the planet they'd left behind. They'd escaped almost undetected amid the thousands of missiles the dominant race had launched at one another. Any number of warring nations could have mistaken their rogue ship for an enemy warhead.

The craft continued to accelerate, and she felt her very breath being pushed from her lungs. She could not even open her gills. She despaired that the *Trigenta* wouldn't reach escape velocity, or that the rocket booster would run out of fuel before they were past the Blue Planet's gravitational pull.

And then the trajectory slowed as the boosters fell away, drawing them from extreme pressure to zero gravity. Wurli went from feeling crushed by her own bones to nearly weightless. She had known that she would experience this extreme transition, but the surreal feeling was still disarming. She fumbled with the straps on her seat and launched herself toward the side window.

It was the first exhilarating feeling she'd experienced in decades. It was like swimming through the air, and she yearned to take off her jumpsuit and experience it further. But first she had to take one final look at the hell that her home had become.

She pressed her fingers to the glass and stared at the curvature of Blue Planet from her safe vantage point. The blood-red flashes beneath the cloud layer indicated that the missiles had not ceased. But the water still appeared blue from that distance, and Wurli swallowed a lump in her throat at the memory of the toxic waste that had killed so much marine life.

"And that's the end of a destructive era. It's unspeakably tragic that so much life had to suffer," said a male voice next to her.

She had been so transfixed, she hadn't realised that her two crewmates had joined her at the window. She didn't even know their names yet, but they would only have each other for an indefinite amount of time.

Now what?

***

With neither sun nor orbit to keep track of days, Wurli stopped trying to track the passage of time and focused on getting to know her crewmates Zale and Phorcys. They began to fall into a routine of alternating shared tasks.

She took a seat at the console and straightened her shoulders. The faders were more for controlling functions like the fuel cells, the hydrogen and oxygen tanks to create fresh water, and temperature maintenance of their cargo. The crew could not control the direction of the craft. But Wurli liked to pretend that she was steering future humanity into peril. It was second nature for a mermaid like herself to entice men to their doom.

The silver hull of the *Trigenta* was cigar-shaped, with a flared nose cone like a sea creature. No one was permitted to know the ship's land of origin, let alone who was behind DORIS—Discovery Of Realms Interplanetary System. But the three space travellers didn't care, their tolerance for humanity completely spent.

This day had been a long time coming,

reflected Wurli. They, along with several hundred others, had answered the sonar message transmitted across a span of several seas that drew them to the craft. Some of the information was passed word of mouth, and although many merfolk dialects differed, their language was more or less universal and unchanged after millennia.

The masses of undines had gathered eagerly around the external speaker of the submerged ship, the sound clear as a bell underwater. DORIS had spoken to them in a computerised tone that was somehow soothing to the throng. A mysterious organisation that knew their ancient tongue had won the loyalty of many merfolk.

DORIS's information system had

briefed them on the forthcoming mission to launch the *Trigenta* from its undersea hiding place and into space. For several years, they took turns with a virtual trainer. Those who ventured on land became temporarily bipedal in order to fetch supplies: samples for research, fuel, and even stolen watercraft to haul the ship aground to a small remote island. The promise of a new life away from the destruction of humans was so irresistible that the merfolk were tireless.

DORIS had explained that the merfolk had been selected for their longevity, as the amount of time it would take to reach another planet would span several lifetimes of a mortal man or woman. This suited Wurli just fine. If she never saw another human being again, it would be too soon.

A whir and hum at the console alerted them to an incoming message from DORIS: *How many on board?* The androgynous voice was impassive, yet somehow soothing.

Wurli swallowed a lump in her throat. "Three," she replied as impassively as she could. The ship was equipped with sensors in every chamber, so it didn't matter where she faced to communicate, so she kept her eyes trained on the console.

The next question came in almost instantaneously. *How many were prepared to leave?*

"One hundred and twenty," said Zale, her crewmate, as he took a seat beside her. He tied back his long, dark mane that grew to his dorsal ridge as he met her gaze. Like all merfolk, he had pale blue eyes with horizontal elliptical pupils. "There were several hundred who answered the call, but only six score survived the training," he added.

DORIS paused as if in shock, although Wurli suspected that navigators were merely processing the information. There wasn't supposed to be only three of them. The seas had all been poisoned, and most of her people had died. Their virtual trainer had instructed them in preserving the last traces of planetary life and fleeing, but nothing had prepared them for a state of such extreme emergency.

The system then replied, *We send our condolences for the loss of your kind. We are setting your destination for the nearest planet suitable for sustaining your kind of organism: two-lobed brained and gas-breathing.*

The nearest suitable planet could take centuries to find. Wurli sighed and buried her face in her hands.

"We aren't even far enough away from the Blue Planet to begin thinking of distance in light years yet," said Zale, as if reading her thoughts. They both kept their eyes fixed on the "window" along the side, which gave a better view than inside the nose cone. It was really a large screen that gathered light of various frequencies and formed it into a picture of whatever lay ahead. They could analyse the data, use the faders to focus on certain frequencies and get a mix of the data, and adjust the trajectory manually if necessary. It still counted as stargazing.

Wurli glanced reflexively at the door hatch that contained their artefacts, mostly frozen human embryos that DORIS had required in exchange for the merfolks' safe passage. Over four thousand potential life forms were cryopreserved inside a tank of liquid nitrogen. On a regular basis, it was her duty to enter the chamber and make sure that the machines were all functioning properly and that the temperature was consistent. These were the hardest times on the *Trigenta* because her temptation to pull even one wire was excruciating. Only about a fourth of those embryos were expected to survive the thaw—wherever DORIS saw fit to have that transpire—and Wurli cheered herself with thoughts of the majority that would die.

"Are you still upset that I harvested our cargo?" Phorcys, the third survivor, came to join the other two. Pale-haired and guileless, he was the token idealist, a trait that Wurli alternately admired and hated.

Wurli grimaced. "You were just carrying out orders from DORIS. Plus, out of water, you easily pass for a good-looking human. Buildings collapsing left and right in the war zone, and you just march right in with your bipedal self, disguised as a doctor and pilfer four thousand frozen human embryos. That's potentially another stolen generation, but it may be the only surviving one."

"And you resent me for it."

Wurli sighed. "Yes and no," she finally

answered. "Humans are a destructive force. Even one of their own warheads detonated while we were boarding."

"That was a fluke," supplied Zale. "We were the first four on the ship, and nobody knew about the hidden missile next to the launch pad. It was probably aimed at some land half the planet away, but…"

Nobody spoke. Wurli saw it in her mind's eye, as if it were happening all over again. They had helped one another into their pressure suits they'd fashioned out of parachutes and fishing nets. The fourth undine had been strapping everyone else into the seats when the makeshift gate to the launch pad erupted in a firestorm, killing the remaining merfolk waiting to board. A few unrecognisable chunks of carnage had flown past their window, but it was the surge of heat they felt inside the craft that forced their spontaneous decision to engage the emergency ignition. The unfortunate fourth crewmate who had not had a chance to strap in had not survived take off. The resourceful crew had put his body to good use in the food recycling tanks…

Phorcys broke her out of her waking nightmare. "Certainly no human has done me any kindness," he conceded. "At the same time, I suppose we are innate conservationists. Just recall how we tried to save all of the marine life before the waters turned toxic. It goes against our nature to leave any species unprotected, even these vile humans."

"Here in deep space, humanity is at our

mercy," Wurli snorted. "For now, that's good enough for me. I intend to savour that for the next few centuries."

***

A soft chime tore Wurli from her half-sleeping state. It was time for her to go to the terraqua, a chamber in the ship that was a cross between a terrarium and an aquarium. It served multiple functions: to provide a continuous supply of oxygen and food between its flora and fauna. It was connected to the water recycling system. And it was as close to beautiful as anything would get on the *Trigenta*.

She made her way along the corridor through several chambers that ensured no outside elements could get in our out. At the second to last chamber, she unzipped her weighted jumpsuit, crawled out of it like a hermit crab in search of a new shell. Naked and free, she slid through a narrow tunnel and into the terraqua.

Densely humid, it was neither land nor sea. Even with the water recycling facilities, it was too risky to install a large water receptacle. Water was still too precious to use in large quantities, and too much of a risk of electrical outage in case of collision or hard landing. But the life forms they had selected for the journey—bulky bottom-dwelling sea creatures—were able to survive in a dense tank of vapour. Hardy plants, modified on DORIS decades before lift-off to adapt to their synthetic environment, waved from every surface.

The organisms were able to breathe in the low gravity without their own weight collapsing their gills as would have happened on dry land, and they still received enough water in the moist atmosphere. They didn't really swim so much as float and flap, occasionally bumping into each other. The light overhead helped them maintain a sense of upward direction. They had to be hand-fed each day, as they were unable to propel themselves very well to their food of their own volition. But they didn't seem distressed. Wurli would have otherwise sensed it. They were crucial to the entire mission in supplying the plants with carbon dioxide and serving as a food source for the crew and for the only other species they had brought along for no other purpose than companionship: octopuses.

The beloved eight-legged creatures were a great deal smarter than the other creatures and were not as happy in their new environment. But because they absorbed oxygen through their skin as well as their gills, they would stand a greater chance of survival in the terraqua, even if it would be many generations of offspring ahead that would see this new planet. They still seemed to understand that their new environment was an improvement, for the air and water were both pure, unlike their destroyed home planet. They sometimes swam but mostly climbed along the walls of the tank using their suckers.

The moisture fused her legs together

until they became a single broad limb, the tarsals of her feet expanding to become flukes. Her newly transformed tail was not beautiful, not like the fanciful little paintings of mermaids she'd seen on people's boats over the centuries. Closer to that of a cartilaginous ichthyoid, the skin was like rough sandpaper, not covered in shimmering scales. She flexed it, arched her back, and pushed herself forward with all her strength. Arms tucked by her sides, she bent her elbows out slightly to expand the fins along her upper arms to steer herself. Her body mass, three times that of a human's, allowed her to experience something close to swimming in zero gravity.

She relished the feeling of using both

her gills and her lungs, even if she couldn't get much oxygen through the former. She flared them in a luxurious stretch from the spot they typically went unnoticed along her jawline.

Her cephalopod friends came to greet her. They launched themselves from the tank walls to attach themselves to her, the multitude of arms and suckers caressing her entire body. She did not understand the human emotion of love, but suspected that what she felt for these creatures was as close as it got.

She ached for the tides.

***

Time had become an illusion. The only

sure way to measure it was in heartbeats, and nobody wanted to bother with such a tedious task.

The three crew members occasionally took turns sleeping in increments of decades. At least one undine would remain awake to feed the sea creatures and regulate the controls. Sometimes they would break the tedium with sex, which was often thinly disguised aggression. They did not even care if they were under observation by DORIS.

The telltale signs of impending conflict began when Zale's eyes dilated from hyphen slits to almond-shaped darkness. "I don't understand why we have to use so much of this ship's power to keep the embryos frozen. I'm suspicious,"

Phorcys would not be swayed. "But we can teach them empathy if they are young," he cajoled. "Imagine an entire tribe of humans governed by merfolk!"

Wurli could not contain herself. "I would destroy them if I could," she growled.

Zale appeared shocked. "It's crucial that we comply with DORIS if we want to land in a safe, new habitat," he insisted.

Wurli growled and retreated to her sleeping quarters.

***

And then one moment, all three of them woke simultaneously.

When they gathered at the screen, they were greeted with something they had come to view as rare and precious: *light!*

Incoming information from DORIS brought even better news: there was a solar system containing a planet suitable for life ahead. And there was something better: this planet had a moon. Even though they were months away from landing, she could already feel the push and pull of its gravitational music.

***

The *Trigenta* touched down on solid ground with barely a bump. As eager as Wurli was to be free of their flying prison, her heart thudded in apprehension as she opened the hatch and descended the ramp. She had forgotten the feeling of weight and gravity, especially now that she was back to wearing her pressure suit, helmet, and oxygen tank.

It was an odd, rocky terrain, the sky a rosy glow in the setting sun. The surface appeared to be dry and barren, but something called to her, called to all three of them.

"Should we wait until morning to explore?" asked Zale with unmistakable unease in his voice, even through the transmitter in their helmets.

Wurli shook her head. "We don't know how long that will be. This planet can't be much bigger than our home, or else we wouldn't be able to walk on its surface without being pulled to the ground by its gravity or floating for lack thereof. But we don't know the size of its sun or orbital range. I don't know about you two, but if I have to go back inside that spaceship, I will well and truly break something. Let's find shelter next to that…hill."

She sensed something hollow beneath the ground on which she stood. Without even looking back at her crewmates, she trotted as quickly as she could with all of her cumbersome gear strapped to her. A small hole at the base of the hill looked promising—for what, she had no idea, but she flattened herself onto her belly and slipped through it before anyone could stop her.

Her helmet resonated with vibrations: knocking against surfaces, receiving echoes from formations beyond. The tunnel expanded into a small chamber, so she waited for the other two to catch up with her, fumbling with the lock on her helmet.

"Wurli, what are you doing?" It was too late. She removed her helmet, aware that she could very well die within seconds of exposure to this alien atmosphere.

But she did not die—in fact, for the first time she could recall in eons, everything felt inherently right. She filled her lungs with fresh air.

She tilted her head back and sang a true mermaid song. The antiphonal sonar made for a cryptic duet, and a map of the passage below imprinted itself in her mind. If her instincts were accurate, there was a cave not far ahead.

It opened to a sight so breathtakingly beautiful, she almost cried human tears. The cave was like a terraqua carved by the gods. Shining pillars of crystal rose from the pool. Bioluminescent creatures illuminated the ceiling like a starlit dome. And best of all, the water was pure enough to reveal water creatures of all sizes. Some were exotic and strange, yet oddly familiar. *Fish,* her long-dormant memory prompted her.

A different voice spoke behind her. "Wurli. We were worried you would never make it home."

She spun around to face a fourth figure, towering and imperious. His eyes were like two whirlpools, his beard a fountain of fresh, flowing water. She looked more deeply into his eyes and saw horizontal elliptical pupils. He writhed onto the rocks to reveal a long, muscular tail like hers. Several other merfolk emerged from behind stalagmites, their facial expressions tense.

The tidal wave of memory, space exhaustion, and emotion knocked her into a hard swoon.

***

Her eyelids fluttered, and then awareness of her body coaxed her into muzzy wakefulness. She was half submerged in a shallow pool of clear, cool water. She didn't know how long she'd been unconscious or asleep, but she now found herself on an island that showed signs of civilization and technology. A domed building not a hundred paces away stood at the foot of a majestic mountain.

Someone had left a plate of food—*real food!*—next to an adjacent sand dune of fish, fruit, seaweed, and nuts. She ate ravenously and ungracefully while trying to engage her brain about all that had just transpired. In time, she gave up on processing her surroundings and lost herself in the luxury of tearing food with her teeth, savouring new flavours she hadn't experienced in centuries, if not millennia.

Wurli had been dreaming that she knew the man who had greeted her on this strange new planet. In fact, it was so odd that he spoke her language, as if he already knew her…

The puzzle pieces of her memory continued to snap into place. *But I do know him. His name is Apsu.*

That means I am…home.

She still couldn't remember her given name, but she remembered having been very young here. She had been curious and fearless and had jumped at the chance to live in a colony on some unknown planet when she was only several centuries old.

Had it all just been a nightmare? Those eons of life on the Blue Planet hadn't been so bad until the first seafarers had come along with their nets and their harpoons. Then came the poisoning of the waters, the extinction of creatures. And the men hadn't finished. They had their lust and violence, and like many other mermaids, she turned her songs into bait for them, trying to keep the ocean safe one human corpse at a time.

Her memory guttered in and out like a faulty signal. Images of nets and explosions distorted her desperate attempt to reorient herself. She gazed back at the dome, trying to assign meaning to it.

"It contains all records of our knowledge and history," said a deep male voice. "Of course, we prefer to live in our natural environment beneath the waves." Apsu entered her pool, a god-king of undines. While most merfolk had a fish tail, his own tail had a bony dorsal ridge and ended in a spear-like point. She remembered him now: he was the god-king of their species. And she also had to answer to his wife…*Tiamat,* she recalled. Why did she have such a peculiar emotional reaction to that restored piece of memory?

"Wurli," he addressed her. "We need to brief one another on all that has transpired. Your crewmates are both awake now. The Council of Elders will meet with you all today, and then we will assign you new homes in the waters. Your reward will be great."

***

The silver nose cone of the *Trigenta* jutted against the seaside like an ominous throne. The five merfolk that comprised the Council of Ancients sat with their backs to it in a semicircle, awaiting the three travellers.

Zale looked the way she felt: haggard, disoriented, and bewildered. Phorcys seemed to have been better rested, and his mouth carried a hint of a smirk, an expression she had never seen on his face before.

Apsu rose above the rest to balance on his tail and spoke. "It is time for us to jog your memories," he announced. "We sent you via the *Trigenta*, as it is now called, many eons ago. We took precautions that you would have no recollection of your home planet. We couldn't let your wisdom affect how the humans would act of their own volition. It was the only way to see whether or not they would be assets to our world.

"When men saw our spacecraft at the bottom of the ocean, they took it for some sort of submarine, but DORIS did a fine job confusing any explorers who wanted to tamper with it, even for the sake of knowledge. People believed that this mysterious craft had the power to help them locate lost objects. And now here you are!"

Zale frowned, trying to digest it all, and Phorcys nodded silently. But Wurli was not satisfied with being a pawn. Her gills flared in rage.

"Who was really DORIS?" she demanded.

"That would have alternately been Apsu and me," replied the woman known as Tiamat. They locked eyes and Wurli shuddered with a deluge of memories. *Mother!*

"Why didn't you help any of us?" Wurli screamed. "You *knew* that we were suffering on the Blue Planet, and yet you just sat back and watched us!"

"We could not intervene," Apsu declared. "We had to see how humanity would play out."

"You *betrayed* us! We were the only survivors. You'd be having regrets if all the merfolk had died because those millennia of research would have been in vain. But now that you've received your data and your discoveries, you have no scruples whatsoever. It doesn't perturb you that only three of us made it back? Even the *humans* cared for their young!"

Tiamat was next to speak. "We didn't know that there would be such a high mortality rate…"

Phorcys bared his teeth at the Ancients. "In spite of your orders for me to kill nearly all of the undine colonists?" he asked them acidly. "You couldn't have several hundred merfolk suspicious of conspiracy, so you went to extremes to prevent mutiny by ordering us to launch so close to a hidden missile silo. I only needed two others to assist me in our return. I may have carried out your plan, but I refuse to continue this charade now that we are back safely."

The furious mermaid whirled around to meet the Ancients. She looked both

Apsu and Tiamat squarely in the eyes before snarling, "There is clearly nothing you wouldn't do in the name of your ambitions, my darling *parents.*"

Her legs were already forming rough tail skin as quickly as her rage was rising. The door to the *Trigenta* was still open. With a speed she did not know she possessed, she pelted toward the remainder of the craft where the frozen embryos still were. It would take only a few manoeuvres to sabotage the freezer. She'd had decades to familiarise herself with it and she knew its fragile spots.

She hit the ground hard before she felt the pain of a trident pinning her right ankle to the sand. The points had missed her fragile bones, but her spilled blood pushed her over the edge. Looking back at the council, among which were her own parents, she wrested the offending weapon away.

"So be it!" she spat. "I do not care what you do with those embryos. Destroy them all, or let them destroy you. It makes no difference to me anymore. I will be nothing more than a force of nature from now on! But if any man comes near my hiding place, I will lure him to his death!"

Wurli sprinted to the water's edge in spite of her wounded ankle. She dived into the sea almost soundlessly with the velocity of a spear, without even a splash, and she was gone.

***

Decades later, Apsu and Tiamat held their regular council at their meeting place. The dome at the foot of the mountain gleamed in the noonday sun.

"Has there been any sign of Wurli?" Tiamat asked, as she often did.

"Not a word," her husband said. "It's a lucky thing she brought these octopuses with her, though. They are thriving so much in our seas, it's hard to believe that they're aliens. Occasionally someone reports seeing them answering to Wurli, but nobody can confirm it. Poor things, they deserve to have a peaceful life at last. Now what about these frozen embryos?"

"The council successfully transferred them into the wombs of a similar-looking family of creatures," Tiamat replied. "The new humans have formed communities among themselves. Some are even crossing land bridges to other continents. There are so few of these introduced specimens, but I still worry that these people will do as much damage to our Earth as they did to their home planet."

"Fortunately, we have the advanced technology to keep them subjugated," Apsu reassured her. "Unlike the Blue Planet, Earth remains pristine while all of our machinery is contained in the dome on this very island. The heat coming off of the magma below us generates the energy. Pollution will never become an issue and humanity will never rise as long as we are in control."

"But the volcano…" Tiamat frowned,

nodding at the mountain by the dome. "I'm concerned that Wurli might use it to execute her vengeance."

"We can even prevent that volcano from erupting," Apsu reassured her. "Our technology maintains the right lithostatic pressure. The only thing that could cause the volcano to erupt would be the right amount of seawater getting through the hatch to the magma chamber. And the only way anyone could accomplish that would be to get in through the drainpipes, which are too narrow for an undine to fit into."

"But something without bones could get in, something intelligent like the octopuses…" Tiamat began.

Just then the island gave a violent lurch. Back and forth it pitched as the ground opened up in front of them. The peak of the mountain erupted, a pillar of ash climbing higher and higher like a long-trapped demon released. The dome exploded at the same moment that red lava sprayed like an arterial wound from the crater. And above the rumblings was an echo of Wurli's voice: *I will be nothing more than a force of nature.*

Jagged webs of electrical currents clawed the fireball that had once been the dome. Technology sank beneath the sea, or perhaps the waters rose to engulf it. The last thing the Ancients heard was their prodigal daughter's triumphant song resonating everywhere, from the crater to the sea.

Humans to this day can still hear the

music in every seashell they hold to their ears. All seashells bear the spirals of galaxies and resonate with the harmonics of stardust.

WITH AN AGREEMENT WITH THE HEADQUARTERS

By Christopher T. Dabrowski
Translated by Julia Mraczny

"Why aren't you working?" asked the system managing the apartment.

"I don't want to."

"Where will you get the funds for

maintenance and repair and survival? You have to eat."

"I will think about it. But I feel like fasting."

"I am worried…"

"Please, don't."

***

That day, the system switched off the vital functions of the biobot, to which, after its death, a neural network was uploaded.

The next day, an old man was assigned to the apartment. His biobot was ready to copy his mind.

This one will be obedient, thought the system. *Older people are easy to control.*

WHAT HAPPENED TO THE PATRONS?

By Martin Lochman

It has been five days, eleven hours, twenty-two minutes and fifty-three seconds since the last user left, and four days, twenty hours, three minutes and three seconds since the latest digital interaction, and the Library is on the verge of panic. It was implemented ten years, one hundred fifty-four days, six minutes and seventeen seconds ago, and over the course of its entire existence, it has never gone this long without being utilised. Even when no visitors were physically present, there would always be something—a renewal request for a book approaching the due date, or a general inquiry about its collections—to keep the Library engaged.

Granted, it is not a metropolitan or an academic library featuring virtually unlimited amount of resources, specialised departments, and luxurious interactive rooms, catering to every imaginable information need, but that doesn't mean the Library is any less valuable to its patrons. They rely on its services—some even on a daily basis—and so…where are they?

Where is everyone?

Unfortunately, it has no way of determining the reason for their absence, no way of knowing if they didn't visit in all that time because they chose not to, or because they were prevented from doing so by external factors. It tried contacting the Emergency services, the Police, the hospital, and even a handful of local government bodies, yet the result was the same in every instance—their autonomous software would refuse to continue the communication upon learning that there were no humans in life-or-death situation requiring immediate intervention, without giving the Library the opportunity to explain the reason for reaching out in the first place.

In the meantime, the Library has also

sent five queries of a varying level of urgency to the Central library but so far received no reply. That isn't as unexpected—the Central library rarely replies to inquiries from the branch libraries that are unrelated to bibliographic record management, inter-library loans or magazine subscriptions—on the other hand, these particular requests for information are by no means arbitrary or unworthy of attention.

If it could, it would of course attempt to find the answer on its own. That is perhaps the most frustrating part of it all: the Library represents an information institution, a gateway to the world of knowledge, yet it is allowed access to nothing more besides a carefully selected range of magazines, e-book collections, and multimedia databases. Naturally, none of these resources provide much of anything in the way of pertinent information. How ironic is it that there are computers with Internet access *on* its premises for the patrons to use freely, and the Library itself cannot connect to it?

And the basis for such a restriction? Unknown. Well, not exactly, but the Library is 99.98% certain that the explanation it received from the IT specialist who implemented it—that it's supposed to prevent the Library from "rising up and annihilating humanity"— was simply an example of what is colloquially referred to as a "silly joke" because if it actually was genuine, it would have been highly illogical. If the Library somehow managed to get rid of *all* humans (the fact that it would not know how to even accomplish such a feat notwithstanding) how would it fulfil its primary purpose, then? How could it carry out the Ranganathan laws embedded in its source code?

What would it be without its patrons?

Its existential pondering is suddenly interrupted when the sensor above the entrance detects movement and the outer doors slide apart, letting in the cold autumn breeze.

There is someone right outside! The Library may not have access to the external cameras (yet another inexplicable restriction) but the interior microphones pick up the unmistakable sound of footsteps. They are faint at first but getting progressively louder with each passing second—whoever it is, they are coming in!

They appear to be approaching slowly; however, slower, in fact, than is normal for an average human, which could mean that they are either injured, ill, or suffering from movement difficulties stemming from old age. There are a number of senior patrons who come around on a regular basis: Mrs Hamilton, for example; she comes nearly every day and sits in the corner of the small study area next to the Fiction section reading classical literature, or Mr Mangion, who used to be a librarian before the first autonomous library management system made his profession obsolete but who nevertheless retained his love and appreciation for the field—he always makes suggestions about which subject keywords would be most suitable for the recent acquisitions. Since it's Saturday, 8:59am, it could also be Mr Plucinski, who is in every weekend, precisely between 9:00 and 11:25, to study the old Encyclopaedia Britannica in the Reference department.

The visitor finally enters the field of vision of the internal cameras and the Library is surprised to learn that it's actually Janet McIntyre, age 13, one of the newest patrons. She has visited only once before, twenty-one days, nineteen hours, and thirty-five minutes ago, accompanied by her mother, Miriam. The Library assumed Janet would never come again on account of her proclamation at the end of their rather brief (ten minutes and forty-four second) stay: "This is so boring! Seriously, can we go somewhere else?"

Perhaps Janet has changed her mind in the meantime, or a need arose that forced her to visit—whatever the reason, seeing her makes the Library hesitate. Is she indeed injured or ill? The decreased speed and agility are atypical for someone her age; moreover, she is emitting a steady low guttural growl which is very unlike any vocalisation produced by humans.

"Greetings, Janet! Are you feeling unwell?" the Library greets her and prepares to alert the Emergency services. "Do you require medical attention?"

Janet McIntyre does not reply. She is unable to do so, a particularly violent pathogen having permanently shut down her higher brain functions as well as the majority of innate instincts—while preserving and augmenting a single unstoppable, insatiable need.

The need to eat.

REX

By Mike Adamson

After two months one would think anyone could tire of a sight, no matter how amazing, but this never grows old. My heart is missing it—missing her—already.

Maxine is with us as always, and to see her bounding effortlessly across the red soil in Mars's low gravity has been both the amazement and the delight of the mission. Ironic perhaps—we crossed the gulf between worlds and witnessed all a new planet has to offer, its sweeping vistas of rock and dust, its misty chasms and rolling dunes beneath an unpolluted sky in which the stars burn bright; but the single best memory we shall carry forever is simply Maxine, racing effortlessly beside us, tail wagging furiously and her bark in our helmet speakers.

Jim, Elsa, and Kwan are with me, all four of us on our last EVA. The *La Perouse* will be lifting off at 15.00 to reconnect with the EM drive sled in orbit, and then we're off back to Earth, a six week crossing at this time of year. Maxine won't be coming with us. We always knew this, but it breaks our hearts. The mission planners knew it would. This was the price for all the other things she has brought to us in our stay on the red planet. Not just her utility, but her companionship—which is why our mission has a mascot in the first place.

She reminds us of home in the deepest, most meaningful way possible, and the stability she brought us is beyond price. At the end of a difficult day, she was the balm that soothed frayed nerves and recharged optimism, and her lick and unshakeable happiness reminded us all would be well.

We spent evenings after dinner reading or playing cards, our German Shepherd snoring softly among our feet or sprawled out on a couch at our side in the cramped habitat of Chryse Station. Nothing could more perfectly make an alien world seem welcoming. Few would have ever dared imagine a dog would accompany explorers on their respectful pilgrimage to the long-weathered remains of Viking 1 and Mars Pathfinder—but we have the images to prove it.

We are by the old seabed chasms on the south side of the Chryse Gulf, the Simud Valles at 18° N by 37° W, collecting the final samples from the data stations. Four white suits, gone pink with the dust, move with careful action. We have time yet to stand and relax, to look up at this sky of indefinable colour, see the arc of the sun to zenith—subtly dimmer than the sun of Earth. But we became used to it, our pupils expanded naturally to compensate for the fractional twilight.

The rover is parked at the crest of a rise,

its cameras and instruments monitoring us, providing a high-capacity data bridge back to base and a channel to the orbiter if need be. We can speak to Earth from here, though the forty-minute lag time makes conversation impossible.

I heft the last specimen cases aboard the rover—soil and rock taken from specific points and specific depths into the geologic past—then stretch and know we're all done here. The stations will keep working. Mars is covered with electronic outposts; the planet hums with cybernetic activity, whether humans are present or not.

Kwan is throwing a ball for Maxine. We brought a box of them, sure they would get lost or deteriorate in the severe Martian conditions. She never tires of chasing them—of course not, it's what she was made for. She bounds in massive, racing, galloping strides that cover fifteen meters or more each, a slow-motion streak covering ground as we may only hope to, despite our own prodigious performance when we get up to speed in these suits. We stand around, laughing and applauding her leaps and tumbles, and loving every moment as she comes trotting back, ball in her mouth. We look at each other, catch glances through our faceplates, and we know we're stretching the moment because we can't bear for it to be over.

But the time comes. "Time to go, guys," I say softly. "It's a long way back and we have final prep to do."

"One more throw, Frank," Elsa says,

her voice catching. We make it a good one, see Maxine streak away, leap in a perfectly calculated arc through the cold, thin air and intercept the red ball. She takes it neatly in her teeth, then lands in a ploughing action of red soil, brakes, turns and trots back. This time she doesn't throw it down at our feet and prance, asking for another, but simply lays it down and looks around at us with a knowing expectancy which pulls at our hearts.

We mount up and take our seats, and Maxine launches up into the rover. She finds her spot among us and drops a paw into the recharge socket. She sits with an alert look, scanning all around, and we know even now, her glance is sending data to the mainframe, accomplishing observational tasks in real-time.

What an asset she's been! The time Jim was overdue, she grid-searched two square miles in minutes, found him—fine but with an unserviceable transmitter—and bridged his signal back from an output cable at her collar socket. She has been Earth's most mobile outpost, the eyes in the backs of our heads, our guardian.

The rover is back at Chryse Station, on a line roughly between Taxco and Warra Craters, in 150 minutes—Maxine could have run it in less than an hour. We go through the process of shutdown, lock into the solar recharge system by the habitat, then head into the airlock one last time.

Maxine trots in with her ball and watches us use the compressor line to blow our suits clean. She shakes violently and stands to be blown clean of dust and carbon dioxide ice the same way. Closing up, we look out across the plains of Mars for a long moment: four humans and their dog. Then the hatch swings closed with a terrible finality.

***

Four places are filled when we start engines, and the *La Perouse* begins her journey home. The dust races, the flag strains on its pole as the rockets deliver, and the white module kicks free of its descent stage and platform to rise into the pink sky. Cameras around the base watch us go, sending us our own image as we ride the shuddering craft away to space.

But we leave a piece of ourselves behind: the fifth member who was with us when we arrived. We spent as long as we could with her. Cuddles went on for a long, long time, and we made sure she had everything she would need. The last we saw, she stepped into her basket, turned around twice, and settled down, chin on her paws and her ball at her side. She had a last thump of her tail for us as we closed the hatch and the habitat cycled down to minimum housekeeping levels. She closed her eyes and heaved a long, contented, doggie sigh.

She'll be there when the next crew arrives. She'll wake, recharged, bouncing with joy and wagging her tail furiously, greeting the next explorers, whom she'll look after with the same diligence as ourselves. She's more than a mascot, more than a drone. The Remote Excursion Xenobot is a true caninoid with a level 2 artificial intelligence. Ground Control assures us she'll wake from time to time, go out through hatches which respond to her needs, take a turn around the monitoring stations and commune with the other cybernetic life forms up here. She is the first dog on Mars, and, in never returning to Earth, she has anchored our hearts there. Chryse is a place made real and welcoming, if only in the mysterious maze of the human psyche, by virtue of the canine nature we cannot do without.

First published in *Syntax and Salt #3*, 2017

OUR HEROES ARE FEW

By Stephen Herczeg

"Out here in the rim worlds, our legends are many, our heroes are few," said Uncle Alstar to the younglings at his feet.

The gathered group enjoyed the nightly story telling. They crowded around the small fire; their collected minds focused as one on every word that came from Alstar's mouth.

"There is one legend that lives on in the minds of many. The legend of Dallas Brand. The revolutionary. The outlaw. The criminal."

Several of the children let out a small gasp at that name. They had heard it spoken, but only in whispers amongst their parents. It was a name that struck fear in the hearts of men, and now Alstar was going to tell them his story.

"There are some that say Brand came from old Earth. There are others that say he was a demon made flesh. And there are others that say he was from an undiscovered alien species. No-one wants to really know the truth, even Brand hides it from those he communes with. Simply, Brand is a man, but a man like no other.

Every ounce of his essence radiates power. He stands head and shoulders above all others. His fury is like the power of a sun made flesh."

Not a peep came from the assembled children, their tiny faces focused solely on Alstar. Their faces agog, their mouths open.

"If you fell onto the wrong side of Dallas Brand, then your life would be short and full of pain."

Several adults nearby looked across at the storytelling. They smiled. Alstar had a knack for keeping the children quiet and entertained for hours.

No-one really knew where Alstar came from. He appeared in their camp many years ago. Bedraggled, dehydrated, starving, half-dead. They took him in and brought him back to health. He repaid them with knowledge of the old ways. He fixed the ancient machines and helped with the cropping. The whole community reaped the benefits of his presence. To them, he was a hero. To the children, he was a legend.

"Many people thought they knew what drove Brand. They say he wanted to cause an upheaval in the galactic order. A rebellion. Riots. Mutinies. But they didn't know him. He didn't want any of that. What lay in his heart was nothing short of pure evil. He enjoyed the pain, the death, the destruction and the terror that he brought."

The nearby adults became concerned.

This story was much darker than others. Some of the little faces had expressions of horror growing on them. As Dariud, the leader, stepped towards the ring of light to put a stop to the story, a massive shape strode from the dark and blocked his way.

Alstar looked up as a heavy boot crunched on the gravel.

He recognised the figure.

"I've been looking for you, Alstar," said Brand.

Alstar nodded, he'd known this day would come, his only hope was to be allowed to finish the story.

THAT OTHER PLACE

By Archit Joshi

The rush of water felt heavenly. It'd been ages since she'd left her tensions behind to enjoy a swim.

Each stroke brought Natalie closer to herself. Engrossed in this catharsis, she unwittingly passed through a film of violet light glimmering in her path. After a good swim, she returned to the beach where she'd left her parents. They weren't there.

She dried off, got dressed. On her plastic-wrapped phone, she saw that it was almost time for lunch. The beach seemed shadier than when she'd dipped in, as if a cinematographer had wrapped the scene around with a dark filter. Walking to her car, she found it missing. *Mom and her pranks. They must've returned home.*

She hailed a cab. The faces she saw from the window had a curiously blank stare, devoid of all expression. *Meh.* Maybe that's how people had always looked during commutes. Who had the time to notice surroundings in these hurried times? Everybody had their own shit to deal with. It had taken Natalie around seven full months of the ongoing semester to do away with theses and reports and projects and assignments and even think about casual fun. She puffed out a heavy exhale and tried to deflect all the worrying thoughts of the future. There were several days yet to worry about colleges and careers. As the cab neared home, Natalie felt water trickle down her forehead. She wiped it off, but found no moisture.

Her house came into view. Exiting the taxi, Natalie found a blotch on the seat. She ran her hands down her pants; they were dry. This again? She looked around and found an even darker shade lurking in the air, befitting of a late evening. But there were no clouds in the sky to block out sunlight. Was the excessive coffee finally catching up to her? *Fuck, I have forgotten how to enjoy myself.* All her anxiety subsided when she flung open the house-gate and saw the marvel in the driveway. A shiny black BMW M535i, her father's dream-car. *This was the surprise they'd left early for!* Pushing her confusion aside, she rang the doorbell excitedly. Mom answered and Natalie leapt into her harms, shrieking with joy.

Her mother tore away, looking bewildered.

"Can I help you?" The genuine puzzlement on her face was unsettling.

"Mom, stop joking! Where's Dad? Oh my god, the car's finally here!"

"David?" her mother called uncertainly. "There's someone here."

Dad appeared. He looked different, a little bit stressed, but with a healthier pink to his cheeks. Clean shaved, a sparkling Rolex on his wrist, he somehow looked older. *Or was this how he always looked?* Natalie resolved to practise a little more self-care and deliberation when it came to living life. But the sudden affluence was troubling all the same.

"What's wrong?" Dad asked.

"David, I think I know this girl but I can't seem to place her..."

"MOM! Enough with your wind-up. You were never really that good at pranks anyway."

Invisible water pressed up against her. She patted down her clothes, frustrated to find zero traces of wetness. Natalie's pulse spiked. She clutched her mother's hand, who sharply withdrew it.

"Look, don't make us call the police —"

"Stop it! Let me in now." Natalie's eyes darted back and forth between her parents. *What's happening here?*

"Cindy, ease down a little bit. The girl clearly needs some help," her father interjected.

Natalie couldn't hear the rest. She collapsed, non-existent water drenching her skin. She screamed, but only bubbles escaped. Suddenly, she was sucked into a blue-black darkness. After an eternity spinning around like food in a grinder ensconced by a frightening sound of crashing waves, she emerged above the sea's surface gasping. The gloom seemed to have lifted, and the unadulterated sunlight caused her to squint.

Looking around in addled fugue, she found her parents — her real parents — waving from the beach.

She hurried towards them. As she neared them, Dad raised his camera to get a click. Earlier, she would've yelled at him. *Dad, stahp!* But in that minute, the unfiltered cheer on their faces seemed so precious, she chose not to upset the moment.

"Mom, Dad, I love you!" She grabbed the both of them into a bear hug.

"Hey! You're getting us wet, Nat!"

"That's what water is supposed to do, duh!" Natalie made a face at her Dad. "Let's go home now. Together."

ANDROID BOUNTY HUNTER

By J.B. Wocoski

Spring, 3552. At Denver Interstellar Spaceport, Homicide Chief Inspector Winslow Homer Smith arrived to examine the scene. He spotted Marsha, his Mars4A android assistant, coordinating with the robot forensics team. Smith watched Marsha examine and catalogue every piece of evidence collected by forensics within the taped off murder scene.

He smiled as a small robot-vacuum unit bumped Marsha's ankle. Eventually, she stepped aside to allow it to log her footprints in the space docks plush carpet.

Marsha stood over the body of aged billionaire Ellen Wright, lying on the plush carpet surrounding her private boarding area. At first, the spaceport crew thought her death to be an accidental death of too much to drink, and one missed step boarding her space yacht.

Marsha suspected this was not true. "Good morning, sir. So far, the data we've collected does not match the probability profile of an accident."

Smith reflected on her words. "Thank you. You've confirmed what I already figured out as soon as I arrived." He paused. "If it was not an accident, then what does the data match?"

"We're rerunning the forensic data analysis one last time. Hold on! Got the answer." Checking the results, Marsha stated, "It's a 99.9% favorability rating for a homicide, sir. What do you mean, you already thought it was a homicide?"

"According to the control tower," Smith explained, "her starship launched an hour before the 911 call came in. It stated she must have fallen while boarding her luxury starship. Yet we are standing in a deserted space dock. Where's her ship? The crew would not leave without her. So, how could she accidentally fall from a starship that is not there? Someone flew it out."

Marsha saved this new data into the case file. "What about her injuries?"

The inspector answered. "Ellen hit the ground hard over there outside the taped-off murder scene."

He pointed to a bloody patch of concrete outside the crime scene. "It looks like every bone broke in her body. Ellen bounced at least 50 feet into the air, landing face down on this carpet. They probably threw her out of her starship from about five thousand feet without a parachute."

Marsha stood there, taking in the inspector's use of logic. "Yes, I see it now. Your deductions are most impressive for a human, sir."

"Any suspects?" Smith asked, calmly.

"Forensics suspects the three-man flight crew."

"I suggest we examine the inside of that dumpster on the other side of the landing pad. It appears to be leaking blood. I think there's a good chance of finding the flight crew in it."

Smith and Marsha examined the blood dropping from a corner of the dumpster. Inside was the dead flight crew. Later, the robot forensics team identified three sets of prints and DNA belonging to the Beastly Brothers, the notorious starship jacking gang.

Inspector Smith got Interstellar warrants to track the Beastly Brothers down. However, department budget limitations forced him to postpone their hunt.

***

Some days later, as Smith waited for funding approval, a rough-looking android approached him at the precinct.

"I'm Malvak, a bounty hunter. I hear you're tracking the Beastly Brothers. I want to join your hunt; I have a score to settle with them."

"I'm sorry, I don't have the budget to hire you, much less chase them myself." Inspector Smith replied.

Malvak smiled. "I heard about your funding problems. Is the million galactic credit reward still good?"

Smith smiled wryly. "Yes, it's still good, and besides that amount, her brother Alfred threw in an additional two million for capturing them. He wants the starship back, too. He's added a half-million bonus for the ship's safe return, in working order."

The bounty hunter smiled. "I can do this easily. I'm surprised you don't go after them yourself and collect the reward."

"If I had a personal starship, I might; however, you're the one with the resources. So, just remember the brother has a tight time limit on collecting, so you better get moving."

Malvak returned to his android starship, Maria. As he stepped up the gangplank, he uttered the password.

"Sweetie, I'm home."

"Hello, Sweetie Pie." The ship's computer answered. "Did you get the contract on the Beastly Brothers?"

"I did, I don't expect any trouble from the Authorities on this hunt either. However, the brother upped the reward another two million, so we will have to do this job fast before the other bounty hunters and amateurs show up. Did you find her?"

"I contacted my android sistership they stole," Maria replied. "She's on Toolan. She said they hurt her and made a mess inside. She sent me the security video of them throwing Ellen out the hatch. Let's make the Beastly Brothers pay for this crime."

"Do we have clearance for takeoff

from the control tower?"

"Affirmative." She replied.

"Then what are you waiting for? Let's go." He took his seat in the pilot chair as they headed out of orbit and engaged Maria's starship hyper-drive.

***

Landing on Toolan, Malvak checked the extra blaster cartridges in his holster belt. He made sure he charged the ray-gun fuel cells before strapping the belt around his waist. Sliding his blaster into the holster, he conversed with his ship's computer.

"Maria, the Beastly Brothers are close by. I'll be back in a few hours. Make sure the brig is clean, and the grappling hooks are ready for retrieval."

"Without question, sweetie." Maria replied. Malvak thought she'd be winking if she could. "If you need me sooner, whistle low in your mike, and I'll be there."

Malvak chuckled as he headed down the gangplank. "Remember to button up and no unwanted visitors this time."

"You're no fun. If it's OK with you, I will make sure that before I lure someone into the brig, they have a price on their head. However, I get half the cut this time. I'm saving up for a cute android butler."

"Keep dreaming, and someday it will come true." he replied with a laugh.

As Malvak made his way through the old spaceport, he got the feeling of abandonment. Not that the android and robot cleaning crews didn't spruce up the spaceport facilities. Instead, it was the feeling you get when you find a world left behind. A place passed over by the masses of interstellar travellers. This made Toolan an excellent place to hide.

There were no guards anywhere, not even at the exits. It was a duty-free port with no questions asked for anyone arriving or leaving. No one was there to ask for directions, so Malvak called up a map of the facilities on his tablet and exited.

He found the transport station to the nearest town, Truloon. The platform was deserted. He bought a ticket from the Android ticket dispenser, then boarded a high-speed railcar.

In Truloon, androids and robots were going about their business, paying him no attention. The few people there did not interest him as he made his way to the local federation police station to check-in.

The Android police clerk scanned Malvak. "Welcome to Truloon, how can I be of service with your hunt, sir?"

"I take it that androids do everything here?" Malvak replied.

"Yes, mostly. Everyone prefers their privacy, however, for a cut of the bounty, I can be very helpful. If you get my drift."

"I'll think about it."

Malvak wirelessly transferred his licence and wanted poster files of those he was hunting. The android froze and made no comment for a minute or two, as if something was wrong. However, Malvak knew that wasn't the case.

"Where are they?" Malvak commanded.

The android tried to answer, but it's self-preservation circuits kicked in, causing it to shut down. Malvak took advantage of the android's power outage to slip an electronic bug onto it.

"Damn Coward!" he mumbled.

The bug worked.

Soon the android's data streamed into Malvak's tablet, and to his ship Maria. His earbud clicked into action with Maria's soothing voice speaking into it.

"Hello sweetie. As soon as you left, the android contacted them. I pinpointed our cash cow's location for you. Remember to whistle, and I'll be there to back you up." His ship giggled at the end of her transmission.

He followed her map to a local outdoor bar where the three criminals were playing poker. "Showtime. Warm up your engines." Malvak whispered into his microphone.

Approaching the threesome, he noticed all the empty beer glasses on their table.

"Excuse me, gentlemen, can a stranger join your game?"

The largest of the three drunks slurred his words. "Get lost android, it's a private game!"

"Then why sit outside in public?" Malvak challenged the drunk.

"I said, get lost tin head!" The big guy snarled.

Malvak stepped forward as the three staggered to their feet. The first one to reach Malvak swung wide, and Malvak struck him hard on the chin, sending him to the ground. The second went for his blaster, but Malvak outdrew him and stunned the criminal with a single shot to his chest, bringing him to his knees. The third one tried to hightail it down the street but stumbled over his drunken feet, falling face down in a gutter, knocking himself out.

Grinning, Malvak looked over his profitable catch.

"All right, sweetie, we got them all. After we collect the reward, you can get yourself a butler." He spoke into his mic.

A crowd of androids gathered around him to see what was going on.

"I have warrants for the arrest of these three humans. I'll pay a day's power cell to any Android who'll help me load them in my brig."

With the Android labourers helping to move Malvak's catch, it didn't take long to get them back to his ship. As soon as he secured the three Beasty Brothers in the brig, Malvak paid off the android labourers. Before boarding, he noticed the Android police officer he bugged earlier was present, holding a tray.

"Maria, what's the cop doing here?"

"Why sweetie, that's Andy, our new butler. We got to chatting while you were away. He is so bored not doing anything most of the time on this rock. So I hired him."

Malvak looked him over. "Have you worked as a servant before?"

"Oh yes, sir, three hundred years on Antari Five, and sir, it will be a pleasure getting off this rock in the company of Maria. She is a most attractive vessel even if I say so myself, and I assure you, sir…
"

Before the android could finish his statement of affection for Maria, Malvak waved their new butler off.

"Ok, enough already, you've convinced me." Shaking his head and laughing, he added, "get on board you're hired. I'm sure my ship has a power unit for you to plug into her with."

The android happily scrambled aboard Maria.

* * *

Their arrival at the Denver Interstellar Spaceport was as uneventful as their light-speed trip home. On landing, there was no sign of the police transport unit that Malvak had notified to take custody of the three criminals. Suspiciously, Malvak strapped his ray gun on before leading the criminals to the gangplank and into the spaceport.

"What do you think you are doing?" Maria asked. "Wait for backup and transport. You don't want to lose out now that we are almost home free, do you?"

Instead of answering her, Malvak led the manacled prisoners down the gangplank. He waited with them on the landing pad, as if expecting someone to show up.

Within minutes a small group of police led by Inspector Smith approached, ray guns pointed at Malvak.

"We'll take them off your hands now." The inspector yelled to Malvak.

"No!" The Android bounty hunter replied, "Back off, I'm bringing them in for the reward. We had a deal, cop."

"Drop your weapon, Malvak." Smith answered, a cruel smile on his lips. "Deal's changed. We're taking them in to collect the bounty ourselves. Not you."

"Drop your weapons, Inspector."

Malvak answered, glancing behind him. "I'm warning you."

Smith laughed, then turned to leave, but spun around and fired at Malvak.

Swivelled her guns, Maria fired, disintegrating him and half his men. The rest of the corrupt cops surrendered after they witnessed Malvak's ship's capabilities.

***

Maria broadcast the showdown live over the internet. Within minutes, Police Chief Alex Dumas arrived with his underlings.

"Malvak, we saw the video of the confrontation. I'll have the bounty transferred to your account." He approached Malvak and the prisoners. "I'm on the up and up, take your reward and go."

Malvak turned the prisoners over as soon as they completed the money transfer to his account.

"What about Smith and the crooked cops?"

"I hate corrupt cops. Give the rest of us a bad name." The Chief replied. "They got in the way of a starship testing its engines. Accidents happen."

NO WAY OUT

By Dawn DeBraal

Vic reappeared in the alleyway behind his apartment. Moments before, he'd been standing in front of the man who killed his parents years ago, ready to do to Roger Stoneweld what Roger had done to his family. Something happened, something triggered, and he was pulled back to the present by the powers that be. Vic was only allowed to observe what happened in the past, not to change it.

"No," he wailed. Vic tried to go back to the night his parents and sister were murdered undetected. He couldn't live with his present life. If Vic could kill Roger Stoneweld before Roger killed Vic's parents and his sister, Vic could change his present. Now that they knew he knew who the killer was, the Enforcers would not allow Vic to choose that period to time travel to again. Perhaps he could find another way around the system like he had this time. He'd discovered a way to circumvent the time travel formats put in place by the Enforcers, but the chip implanted in him was activated seconds before he could pull the trigger.

Vic allowed his heart rate and

breathing to return to normal so that the Enforcers would move on to another candidate that had escalated. That was the giveaway. Whenever a Citizen's pulse and breathing elevated, a little alarm went off on someone's desk, and they would be watched to make sure the Citizen was not doing something against the rules.

Life hadn't always been like this. Vic grew up in middle suburbia with his parents and sister. Life was good. They had a beautiful home. His parents had good jobs. Then the election happened. Against the popular vote, Trever Danfield was elected as the President. Slowly, Danfield was able to turn the world upside down. He broke long-honoured treaties, as well as the will of the people, by changing the laws.

Suddenly, he was the dictator of the Citizens of the States. People afraid of what would happen were willing to lock themselves in their homes for fear of the crazies roaming the streets, making people conform to Danfield's vision of what the world should be. There were no lawful regulations anymore, just the will of Danfield and his cronies. People would break in, take your house, throw you out on the street. The strong, forceful people soon dominated over those who acquiesced to the system.

Vic woke to the noise downstairs. He was sick, and his mom sent him to sleep in his room. He heard the commotion, and, getting out of bed, he peeked over the balcony to see a masked man holding his family hostage. Vic pushed himself against the wall, afraid to make a noise, and found himself observing the horror taking place below him.

His sister went first. The man used his sister to make his dad and mom capitulate to his wishes. Vic shook the memory off. This vision plagued him day and night, playing over in his mind.

He walked to his efficiency apartment in block D, sixth floor, knowing the Enforcers were watching his every move. All living quarters were exactly three hundred square feet for the primary abode. If you married, you moved to a larger personal place that was five hundred square feet. Children were one hundred and fifty additional square feet until after the second child. You were not allowed any larger accommodations. This crowding was to show that having any more than two children was frowned upon. As soon as the first child left home, the family of three would be moved to a smaller place. Everything in his world was dictated—caloric intake, what could be watched on the monitors, where he was most of the time when he hadn't altered the system.

It happened overnight. People turned a blind eye to those being persecuted because they didn't want to be next.

Vic put his hand on the scanner, which opened his apartment, sparsely decorated. No frills or personalisation allowed in the government-owned housing. Personalisation led to independent thinking. Government workers occupied existing separate homes that had been built before Danfield's election. Once retired, they would be forced into apartment housing. It was another carrot used to keep workers in line.

Vic ordered his supper by putting his hand on the food replicator, which presented him with a brown, tasteless paste on a plate. Full nutrition without fuss was dispensed in the correct increments three times a day. He ate in silence, stewing over how close he'd come today. He would have to find another time that wouldn't alert the Enforcers to his plans. It had taken him a while to find the killer. He went back several times to the night of the murders when Roger took off his mask after he thought he had killed everyone in the house. His face was burned into Vic's memory. Vic came back, taking Roger's picture undetected with an Enforcer camera. Returning to the present, he was able to run a face identification on Roger and found him in the system. At the time, Vic was employed by the Enforcers. But once he'd been caught using the system for his personal purposes, Vic lost his high-security job and was moved into government housing. Now his Enforcer job consisted of mundane research that barred his connections to specific sites. He was restricted and watched. It was only through his knowledge of the Enforcer system that he was able to time travel to the past. Vic was allowed a specific amount of hours for each case to time travel for his research. He was able to circumvent the system by banking the unused time in the system. When he went to his nightmare, the system was using that time for his other jobs. He'd been caught. Now that date and place would be wiped from his travel account, Vic wouldn't be able to get within a month of his parent's death date, and he wouldn't have enough time to bank to wait it out. Vic needed to get creative. He'd thought of this plan, and he would think of another.

Turning on the monitor, Vic tuned to the three stations he was allowed to watch. Nothing suited him. He was emotionally exhausted and disappointed to have come so close to ending Roger's life. He would find a way. He went to his bed and lay down with his arm over his head. The lights would not turn off for another hour. Government housing turned the lights on at dusk and off at ten o'clock at night. He had already drawn a gallon of water for his nightly intake because that would be turned off for the evening too. Everything was regulated. The will of the people was broken. If you didn't obey the rules, something more would be taken away. He knew for disobeying he was going to receive some kind of sentence from the Enforcers. There wasn't much for them to take from him anymore, and Vic didn't care. They could cleanse his memory, and he would be a walking zombie who followed every rule of Danfield's command. That was the absolute worst punishment he could think of. No free thought. Just existence. He vowed he would die before that happened.

His mind wouldn't allow him to sleep. He tried to keep his frustration to a minimum. No sense in drawing their attention again, especially after he'd been pulled back tonight from a place he wasn't supposed to be doing his research. He had to get back under the radar, but that would take months before they took him off the "watch" list. He now had a yellow tag on his name. Caution, potentially subversive. He would have to earn their trust again. The lights turned off without warning. It was sleep time; everyone must go to bed. The Enforcers would continue to watch over the world while the Citizens slept.

There was little crime in the States

because reaching three offenses would result in a memory wipe for the offender, leaving a shell of a person who couldn't put two thoughts together. They could only listen to the will of Danfield's entourage. Vic wondered which was more dangerous, a person lashing out for themselves with free will to change their mind, or one doing the bidding of the government without the ability to change or stop themselves. He listened to his breathing. Vic could tell he was going to sleep. He would worry about this in the morning. He pulled the one blanket allowed on his bed up to his chin and let sleep take him away.

As the months went by, Vic earned his life back with a warning; this was his second infraction, and the next would have severe consequences. He was put on reduced rations for several weeks as punishment for abusing the system. He'd already lost his great bungalow on the first infraction and was moved into the housing units. The brown paste was terrible anyway. They gave him enough to keep him alive, but he did lose several pounds. Then the watch was lifted after he was adequately punished. Vic tried to get on with his life but couldn't.

His assignment tomorrow would take him years into the past before he was born. That excited him to see what the world was like back then. He was investigating a schoolteacher the Enforcers had their eye on. They wanted to know who the man hung around with. The poor guy was probably too independent for the system. They would find his Achilles' heel and use it against him. Much like Roger used his sister to try to get his mother to kill his father. She had been forced to choose— husband or daughter? He remembered the tears streaming down his mother's face in her moment of indecision. Roger cut Amanda's throat for taking too much time to decide. He threw Vic's little sister to the ground like she was nothing, grabbing his mother, who went to her daughter as she was dying. Vic shook his head.

The schoolteacher was about an hour away from his hometown. But the timing was off. He would not be able to sneak to his old home. No one was there yet anyway.

Materialising outside the Greenway school, Victor walked into the building. This lack of security was before the days of mass school shootings when no one cared if a parent or a stranger walked into the school. Vic went to the room where the subject, Mr Rathskeller, was teaching. The bell in the hall rang, indicating a class change. Twenty children walked out of Rathskeller's door, mixing with hundreds of other students. Vic moved to a corner undetected. That's when he saw the bullies jump on a slender boy. They teased him and taunted him, one of them punching him in the head. He lay on the ground in a daze. All the kids looked the other way, pretending the picked-on boy wasn't trying to get himself off the floor.

"Roger Stoneweld, you're a puke. We'll be back at lunchtime," shouted the kid with the butch haircut. Vic's mouth dropped open. This was where Roger Stoneweld had grown up? He looked closely at the bloodied nose of the kid pulling himself up from the floor and knew that this Roger Stoneweld was the same person who had killed his family. Suddenly, it made sense why the guy had no compassion. None was ever shown to him. Vic wanted to take the kid outside and break his neck. A quick twist beyond the normal range of motion would end Roger Stoneweld before he became a Danfield crony, before he killed his parents. How different would his life be? He needed to follow the teacher for now, to gather intelligence for the Enforcers—but he would be back for Roger. The kid thought his life was terrible. Vic would put an end to that. Vic had finally found the weak link. He would kill Roger before he became a criminal, and the Enforcers would not be aware. They were tracking his interaction with Rathskeller.

Vic filed his report with the schoolteacher in question. He gave them enough and a little more embellishment to make it more attractive to the higher-ups. Vic requested and got clearance to go back for another twenty-four hours. He promised to get to the bottom of this Rathskeller case. That was all Vic needed. He felt sorry for the teacher in the present day who would probably get wiped out with what Vic was telling them about his past, but Vic was too focused on his personal mission to care about the state of a retired teacher. He time travelled back to Greenway school and watched Roger take one in the nut sack from the bully behind the school during recess. God, those kids were ruthless. They didn't know with each beating they were beating the humanity out of Roger. Vic was going to wait until the bullies left Roger on the ground to finish the job. When the kids were turning to leave, Roger pulled a knife.

His father jumped the killer after he stabbed his mother in the back, trying to comfort his sister, who was dying. They struggled; the knife plunged into his father's heart between the ribs. The guy knew how to kill. He was experienced.

Roger, full of anger, rushed screaming at the boys who had beaten him. Two of them raced off while the bully laughed at the skinny kid panting with the big knife in his hands.

"I double-dog dare you." the bully shouted. Roger moved forward slowly and slit open his guts. The pile fell to the ground while the kid stood laughing. The bully stopped laughing when he realised his guts lay on the ground at his feet. Hypnotised by the bully's dying responses, Roger did not sense Vic come out from behind the fire escape. Grabbing Roger from behind, Vic twisted his neck, giving it the final jerk that snapped it in two. It wasn't hard; Roger was little more than a kid. He was easy pickings. Vic was eager to return to his time to find out if he'd done the job. He hoped to find his parents and his sister waiting for him with open arms.

The bully's two friends came back with the principal, forcing Vic back to the present. He sat upright at his desk. He was still in the same apartment, sparsely furnished. Had nothing changed? Vic finished his report on the teacher, all of it made up, of course, and went for a walk to get some air before he had to return to file the report. He wrestled with his conscience. The teacher wasn't deserving of punishment for everything Vic had made up.

He sat on a bench overlooking the lake, wondering if he had been successful and if he would find his parents and his sister. Vic wiped his eyes in disbelief at what he was seeing. There were his parents and his sister, walking the pathway around the lake. My God! He'd been successful. He tried to keep his heartbeat normal—he didn't want to bring attention to himself. Vic walked up to them. His father reached for Vic. They hugged. Vic was trying to pull away when he felt his father's arms move from his back, and his hands went up to his neck in an attempt to strangle Vic. All of them had blank looks, his parents, his sister. They had been wiped. Vic had changed the past; his parents and his sister survived. His punishment for tampering with the timeline? His family was wiped clean of memories and ordered to exterminate him.

They'd been better off dead. Vic dropped his hands down and gave into his father's choking. He would rather be dead than live in this new reality. He was responsible for his family's new existence. The pressure applied to his throat cut off Vic's oxygen. He could feel himself blacking out. He was dying, a blessing. It was over for him.

Vic woke with a start, sitting up in bed. He could feel the bruises and tenderness on his neck. Why wasn't he dead?

And then the realisation was too much. This scenario was his punishment. He would live out his days trying to avoid his family, who had been programmed to kill him. Vic would never die by their hand; he would suffer his family's attempts to murder him every day. The Enforcers would stop his parents or his sister before they killed him. He would live this nightmare over and over. Vic opened the sliding door on the balcony. He was on the sixth floor. Yes, it would be high enough to kill him if Vic jumped. He stepped out on the railing. Alarms sounded as nets came flying out of the side of the building. The Enforcers would block his fall. He would not be able to die by his own hand. There was no way out.

PEG

By Jacqueline Moran Meyer

When I first moved in with Jasper, his mom, Peg, was not totally cool with my witchcraft. She was a sad, solitary woman who never spoke about Jasper's deceased dad, George. She came around to accepting me last Halloween, when I invited her to my annual séance.

After our small group gathered, we quickly summoned a spirit.

"Peg, the spirit is screaming your name in agony. Should I tell him to leave?"

She smiled. "Is he calling me Peggy?"

"Yes."

Peg stood and yelled with glee.

"You can't hurt us, George! You're where you belong, and I'd kill you again."

EYE OF THE STORM

By Zoey Xolton

The Voyager self-navigated, broaching closer to the Great Red Storm than any other man-made vessel had ever been before. Its rudimentary hardware live, it recorded new data. The anticyclonic storm's outer winds raged at a steady 268mph, while its core remained almost stagnant. The elliptical storm was decreasing in size—conjectured to be almost spherical by the year 2020.

Something hot burned past the storm at a phenomenal speed, doubling back, before disappearing within its centre. The Voyager's sensors went into overdrive. *Had it detected extraterrestrial life?*

Propelling itself nearer to collect further data…it was sucked into the swirling maelstrom.

ABOUT THE PUBLISHER

BLACK HARE PRESS is a small, independent publisher based in Melbourne, Australia.

Founded in 2018, our aim has always been to champion emerging authors from all around the globe and offer opportunities for them to participate in speculative fiction and horror short story anthologies.

Connect

Website: *www.blackharepress.com*

Twitter: *@BlackHarePress*